The Casebook of
Inspector Armstrong
Volume II

This edition published in Great Britain in 2013 by DB Publishing, an imprint of JMD Media.

Copyright © Martin Daley 2013

All Rights Reserved. No part of this publication may be reproduced, stored in a retrieval system, or transmitted in any form, or by any means, electronic, mechanical, photocopying, recording or otherwise without the prior permission in writing of the copyright holders, nor be otherwise circulated in any form or binding or cover other than in which it is published and without a similar condition being imposed on the subsequent publisher.

ISBN 9781780913285

Printed and bound by Copytech (UK) Limited, Peterborough.

The Casebook of

Inspector Armstrong

Volume II

Martin Daley

In memory of Monsignor Greg Turner

Front cover: Carlisle Races in 1904 – courtesy of Carlisle Library

Rear cover: Lowther Castle – author's own

Frontispiece: Wetheral Station and Viaduct – courtesy of Simon Ledingham

Contents

The Bells & Plate Fix — 7

Case Closed	8
More than a glass of lemonade	14
The Memory of a Good Woman	21
The Box	27
The Contents	32
The Spring Meeting 1909	38
The Spring Meeting 1912	43
Reuben's Stage	48
Down Boundary	53
The Investigation Heads North	58
An Unwelcome Visitor	63
The Fate of Joseph Carter	68
The Tying up of Loose Ends	73
A Painful Discovery	79
An Unpredictable Twenty-Four Hours Ahead	85
The Fate of Cornelius Armstrong	90
The End Game	95

The Kaiser's Assassin — 101

It's War!	102
A Slight Change of Plans	107
Martindale	112
An Unexpected Visitor	118
Lowther Castle	123
The Halloween Ball	128
Curious Liaisons	134
A Busman's Holiday	140
Concerns and Suspicions	145
The Volunteers	151
Reunions and Reflections	156
The Decline of Alex Strickland	161
Suspicions Confirmed	166
The Ticking Clock	170
The Kaiser's Would-Be Assassin	175

The Bells
& Plate Fix

Case Closed

"Inspector..." – Coroner, Charles Appleby, slowly drew out the word as he peered over his glasses at the file in front of him, before looking out into the court for the man who he was about to call – "...Armstrong," he said at last. The dozens present at the inquest hung on his every word, willing him to complete the introduction. Finally, they turned as one to look at the man who was about to be questioned. Cornelius Armstrong walked towards the witness box to report his findings on the death of Joseph Carter.

Inspector Armstrong had been called to the scene of the young man's demise on the last Friday of June, 1911. It was a date he was unlikely to forget, as he had celebrated his forty-seventh birthday the previous day, which also coincided with the coronation of King George V. He found himself sitting at his desk reading about the latter event in the morning newspaper when he received a call to attend the scene of the man's death.

The deceased worked as a solicitor's clerk, and spent his leisure time carrying out the same role – albeit in very different circumstances – for local bookmakers. The timing of his death therefore had taken on extra significance as it had apparently occurred during the city's busiest week of the year, with factories and businesses closing down to celebrate Race Week.

His body had been found lying face down in the water on the east side of Eden Bridge, in the heart of Carlisle. It rested against one of the large piers that supported the five arches, which were widest at their base and had a further stepped construction to the waterline. There was therefore more than one theory as to how the body had entered the water, and what had caused its severe head injuries.

It could have been the case that Carter had fallen – or had been pushed – from the bridge, causing the body to strike its head against the concrete base before bouncing into the water, where it would have been eased back against the pier by the river's current. Armstrong's theory however was slightly different: he believed that the body had been injured elsewhere, and had been placed in the water further up-river before it drifted down to the bridge where it was halted after banging into the base of the pier.

Armstrong's investigation had been hampered from a very early stage by Jack Dixon's report in the *Carlisle Journal*, which suggested that Joseph Carter's fatal injuries had been sustained after he had simply fallen from the bridge, probably whilst under the influence of drink.

But for the Inspector, there were just too many unanswered questions. Why would the young man be under the influence when he was not known to be a heavy drinker and was from a respectable background? Why would he be crossing the Eden Bridge when his lodgings were in the opposite direction on London Road? Why did no one see him fall on such a busy thoroughfare? Why were his pockets completely empty of any contents? As it was the bookies' busiest week of the year – why would he be out at night at all?

Carter's post mortem had been inconclusive and – much to the annoyance of the coroner, who inwardly concurred with the newspaper article – the original inquest had been opened and adjourned, at the request of the police, to allow more time to investigate.

Now, three months on, with Inspector Armstrong leading the investigation, the police had little more to go on than they did back in June. Appleby had begun proceedings by outlining the case once more to the jury, before calling the witnesses.

Doctor James Bell was up first, and he formally repeated his inconclusive findings during the autopsy. He then produced photographs of Carter's body, which were passed to Mr. Appleby and then to the members of the jury. The reaction of some of the gentlemen confirmed the poor boy's head had been horribly mutilated. Bell explained, "I can confirm that the head injuries were the cause of death, but it is impossible to say whether they were caused by accident or design. There is no possibility of drowning as the body had very little water in the lungs," – he explained this comment further – "had there been water in the lungs, it would have indicated that the victim would still have been alive at the point of submersion."

Appleby addressed his witness, "Doctor Bell, I believe the height of the Eden Bridge is in the region of thirty feet – do you feel the injuries are consistent with a fall from that distance?"

"Again it is difficult to give a definitive answer – it is certainly possible, but would depend on the angle of the body as it hit the water or the base of the concrete pier."

After a few more token questions, Bell was thanked and asked to step down. He was followed by the young man's employer, solicitor David Edwards, who testified to the lad's impeccable character; his landlady, Mrs. MacPherson, whose most significant contribution was to inform the court that her tenant always paid his rent on time; and then his distraught older brother John, who spoke movingly of the close relationship the two shared.

Finally, it was the turn of a more nervous than usual Inspector Cornelius Armstrong. His anxiety stemmed from the fact that he had little more proof of foul play than when the court adjourned in early summer. He climbed the two steps into the witness box, took the bible in his right hand, and read the oath held in front of him by the court usher.

As if to give Armstrong a big build up, Appleby began by briefly reminding the court of the evidence heard so far. He then turned to the policeman. Was there a suspect in the case? Was there a motive for anyone causing harm to the young man? Was there any evidence that Carter himself was in some sort of difficulty in his private life – financially perhaps? To all questions, Armstrong was forced to reluctantly answer in the negative.

"Inspector," resumed the coroner," I find your report and your evidence somewhat ambiguous and frankly irritating. On the one hand you are suggesting that there has been foul play in the death of Joseph Carter, and yet you cannot provide any tangible evidence to support this view.

On what do you base your conclusions?'

Armstrong answered Mr. Appleby's latest question in his own mind before speaking – it sounded pathetic even to him. He grabbed the wooden rail of the witness box in front of him. "My own policeman's instinct," he said at last.

There were uncomfortable murmurings and even the odd suppressed snigger from the public gallery. Charles Appleby removed his heavy tortoiseshell spectacles and pinched the bridge of his nose before palming back the wisps of grey hair from his high forehead with an audible exhalation. As he worked the wire arms back around his ears he said, 'I think that will be all Inspector, you may step down."

Cornelius – head bowed in embarrassment – walked back to his seat.

The coroner then addressed the gentlemen of the jury. He reminded them that their task was to determine the circumstances surrounding Joseph Carter's death.

As far as he saw it, there were several possibilities before them, "… but frankly, I do not believe foul play to be one of them. None of the evidence points to any wrongdoing. It could be that Mr. Carter *was* under the influence of alcohol when he fell; it could be that he had been taken ill and that had resulted in him becoming disoriented – this is what may have caused him to fall.

"There is no evidence that Mr. Carter's body was moved to the location where it was found, so we can only conclude that no other party was involved. The final possibilities are that he was startled in some way and lost his footing as a result; or that he committed suicide, either in a premeditated act – planned in the full clarity of mind – or he may have jumped deliberately in the heat of a moment of delusion."

The jury retired, but with such a clear direction from the coroner, it seemed they had little to debate. They returned within half an hour with a verdict of 'accidental death.' It came as little surprise to anyone – including Inspector Armstrong – and after the usual formalities Charles Appleby declared the inquest closed with a bang of his gavel. Chairs grated against the wooden floor as those present stood to allow him to leave. Armstrong sat back down to allow the noisy courtroom to clear.

Three months after the discovery of the body, the disconsolate policeman followed a few stragglers out, full of nagging self-doubt. The coroner's verdict had been delivered; everything that could be said had been said – which wasn't much – and all the while, Armstrong knew he would never get the decision he wanted. He also knew that he would have to face the embarrassment of speaking to Dixon and Cecil Matthews from the *Cumberland News*, who would be waiting outside. The local pressmen recognised Armstrong as the best detective in the Cumberland Constabulary, but that was all the more reason to print a juicy story on the shortcomings in the available resources and judgment of the local force.

It was a blazing August day, one when the sun mixes with the factory-generated pollution to create high, oppressive temperatures to cast a sepia veil over the city. As Armstrong walked through the reception area towards the exit, he saw them through the doorway and slowed his step. He had no wish to discuss the verdict, but he knew that questions and jibes were inevitable. As he stepped outside into the bright sunlight, his pupils shrank to pinpricks in the sudden brightness, and he instinctively raised his hand in protection.

"How do you react to the verdict, Corny?" asked Dixon, with his usual lack of respect for reputation, "does this bring your judgment into question?"

Armstrong raised a placid smile, "I'm sure you will make your own judgment in your newspaper tomorrow." His tone was neutral, knowing that he was in a position of some weakness. "I respect the Coroner's decision, whatever my own feelings."

Before any further questioning, Armstrong saw the deceased's brother, John, and his employer David Edwards standing nearby. Ignoring the journalists, he approached the two.

"Once again, I'm sorry for your loss Mr. Carter. You know my feelings on the death of your brother, but sadly I could not convince the coroner to keep the case open."

The older brother was the stationmaster at the small village of Wetheral, four miles east of the city. During his investigation, Armstrong had questioned John about Joseph's state of mind leading up to his death (had he noticed anything different about his manner or mood?); John was shocked by his brother's passing, and could only offer a token "He was such a quiet, honest lad – I can't believe it," in response to the policeman's questions.

Cornelius now felt that he had prolonged the older Carter's grief unnecessarily by continually suggesting that there was more to the young man's death than met the eye.

"Don't blame yourself Inspector," said John as they stood on English Street in the bright sunshine, "I'm only pleased our dear parents weren't here to see Joseph's misfortune."

Edwards stood in silence meanwhile; he knew no words were necessary.

The three men went their separate ways after a few minutes, none of them believing their paths were likely to cross again regarding the matter.

More than a glass of lemonade

The large round clock hung above the eastbound platform at Wetheral's pretty railway station, waiting for the ten o'clock Carlisle-to-Newcastle train to arrive on the beautiful early spring morning. The platform – like the one opposite – was furnished with gas lamps that stood like sentries at twenty-yard intervals. From their posts hung decorative baskets, flush with brightly coloured primrose and wisps of heather.

Beyond the platform, any eastbound train was destined to traverse the Wetheral Viaduct, the five arches of which towered one hundred feet above the River Eden. Running alongside the railway line, a footpath provided a route for any strong-willed pedestrian to take the journey across to the village of Great Corby, on the other side of the valley.

The stationmaster's ivy-covered house stood adjacent to the platform; in front of its picket fence stood John Carter checking his pocket watch against the time of the clock. The distinctive whistle of the train and the puffs of steam over the tree tops indicated the imminent arrival, and as the train finally came into sight just as the second hand ticked round towards its deadline, Carter gave his watch a satisfied nod.

The train slowed to a crawl, then lurched suddenly to its dead stop. Cornelius Armstrong stepped down onto the steam filled platform and walked towards the footbridge that would lead a visitor to the slight incline towards the village, or the ninety-nine stepped footpath that was to lead the off-duty policeman down to the banks of the Eden, and the purpose of his journey.

As he approached the footbridge, he saw the stationmaster further down the platform and considered whether or not to go and say hello, given his previous involvement some months earlier. As Carter was engrossed in conversation with two other passengers who had descended from the train – and had not seen Cornelius in any case – the policeman thought better of it and climbed the footbridge to cross the track.

For a few weeks – with the improvement in the weather – Cornelius had promised himself a walk along the Eden from Wetheral back into the city, where he hoped to spend a relaxing day spotting as many river birds as possible. The previous months had proved uncomfortable given his humiliation at the Coroner's Court. His colleagues, his Chief Constable, and even the surrounding community thought no less of the Detective Inspector, but his personal pride had been hurt, and the cutting article that appeared in the *Journal*, the day following the hearing, still jarred.

As Cornelius descended the ninety-nine steps, the shrill from Stationmaster Carter's whistle signaled the train's departure. At the bottom, he looked up at the stunning viaduct that towered above him, and then at the river below. The curls of smoke that rolled over the top of the large bridge before dissipating into the sapphire sky were the only indication that the idyllic, pastoral silence had been disturbed.

Cornelius stood for a few minutes on the narrow track that was thirty paces from the river; he closed his eyes and breathed in the fresh air. His reverie was broken by the sound of something softly hitting the ground behind him, and then, almost instantaneously, the object knocking against the back of his leg. He looked down to see a small red ball lying at his feet. He looked round to see where it had come from, and was faced with a large wall, in the middle of which was a wooden door that presumably led to a garden from where he heard muffled voices.

The ball had been accidently thrown by eleven-year-old Edward Stoneycroft, who was playing in his mother's garden.

"Mummy?" called Edward.

"What is it darling?" asked his mother coming out of her greenhouse where she had been preparing some seeds for the forthcoming summer.

"The ball…" replied her son, pointing in the general direction of the large garden wall.

Amelia Stoneycroft hid her frustration, as she always did when her son's learning difficulties often manifested themselves through his carelessness. She walked across the lawn removing her gardening gloves, and descended the four steps to the wooden door that opened on to the road outside. "Sweetheart, you really must try and be more caref...*oh!*" As she opened the door she was faced by a man standing on the road holding Edward's red ball.

"Hello," he said with a smile, "I assume this is yours."

"That's my ball," said Edward as he peeked nervously at the man from behind the white gossamer dress of his mother that was protected by her green gardener's apron.

The policeman felt compelled to explain himself. "I'm sorry, I didn't mean to startle you." He tipped his cap. "My name is Cornelius Armstrong. I was just about to set off on a walk along the river." He raised his binoculars that hung around his neck, "A beautiful day for bird watching," he said, completing his explanation.

The woman smiled, somewhat re-assured. As Cornelius moved forward to hand the ball back to the boy's mother, she looked quizzically at the stranger, "Forgive me, but your name rings a bell with me."

"Perhaps," said Armstrong, "I am a policeman. My name sometimes appears in the local press when there is an important case to report on."

"Ah, that's right – that is where I have seen it. If I'm not mistaken you interviewed Mr. Carter about his poor brother last year. I remember him saying how kind you were."

Before Cornelius could respond, another voice interrupted.

"Would you like some lemonade?" It was Edward again from behind his mother.

Cornelius leant to one side to see where the little voice had come from, "Oh I don't think…"

"It's very nice," persisted the young boy before Cornelius could make his polite refusal. Edward looked to his mother for approval and Amelia – unable to deny the boy anything – acquiesced with a smile.

"Please do," she said turning back to Cornelius, "I'm sure a little refreshment would be most welcome before you start your day's bird watching."

"In that case," said the policeman, "how could I possibly refuse such a kind offer from such a fine young man."

The lady of the house stood to one side to allow her guest through into the garden, and indicated a small iron table with matching chairs sitting on a paved area that was shaded by a high wall of fir trees. "I'm sorry, I should have introduced myself," she said. "My name is Amelia Stoneycroft, and this is Edward."

"Very pleased to meet you both."

"Edward darling, you take Mr. Armstrong across to the table and I will get some lemonade." With that, Mrs. Stoneycroft disappeared into her kitchen through a door at the rear of the house.

Cornelius sat down and admired the large, secluded garden. There was a small meadow area adjacent to the large greenhouse that was peppered with yellow primrose and lesser celandine, with just the odd splash of purple and white crocus. Daffodils lined the perimeter of the garden, while a blossoming cherry tree stood as the centerpiece of the stunning display in the middle of the lawn.

"You have a beautiful garden, Edward," said Cornelius.

"Mummy takes care of it," replied the boy, "Mummy's very good at taking care of things."

It was obvious to Cornelius that the young lad had some difficulties with his speech and coordination. He smiled inwardly as he imagined how his housekeeper Mrs. Wheeler would innocently describe the lad's symptoms to one of her friends (a quick check to her left and right to make sure no one was in earshot, and then the exaggerated mouthing of the words the "Poor la'al lad – he's a bit slow!" whilst simultaneously lowering her voice so as not to offend the omniscient presence). "Well, she makes a lovely job of it," concluded the visitor.

Mrs. Stoneycroft then appeared carrying a tray with a bottle of home-made lemonade, three glasses, and plate of biscuits.

"Please, let me help you with that," said Cornelius, rising from his seat and taking the tray. "Edward was just telling me about your passion for your garden. I must compliment you on the result, it really is beautiful."

"Thank you," said Amelia, pouring the lemonade, "it is my pride and joy I must confess" – and then turning to her son – "we do enjoy it, don't we darling?"

Edward nodded while studying his recently recovered ball. Without prompting, the boy's mother proceeded to fill in a few gaps that had occurred to Armstrong.

"Edward's father works for the North Eastern Railway Company, and spends at least two days each week in Newcastle."

"Is your father away at the moment Edward?" asked Cornelius.

"He works on the railway bridge," replied the boy.

"Edward always associates his father with the viaduct," explained Amelia, "as he catches the train up at the station and goes across the bridge towards the north east."

Cornelius smiled, "It's very tall isn't it?"

Edward continued looking at the ball. "The man fall off the bridge," he said, as much to himself as to his mother and the policeman. The two adults ceased their desultory chat and looked at the boy.

"What's that darling?"

"The man fall off the bridge," repeated Edward.

"When was this, dear?"

"The glass got smashed," he said pointing to the greenhouse, "and the man fall off the bridge."

"When the glass was smashed?" repeated his mother, "that was a long time ago."

The policeman couldn't help himself from enquiring, "Was there some kind of accident?" he asked.

"There was that dreadful storm last year when it rained so heavily we thought the Eden would burst its banks and we would all be flooded. Fortunately it never came to that, but in the high winds part of one of the fir trees broke off and smashed through the greenhouse roof."

"Yes, I remember the unusual severity for the time of year," recalled Armstrong. "There was a lot of damage to buildings in the city if I recall – slates blown off roofs and the like. It was late June wasn't it?" he asked, almost to himself.

"That's right, it was," agreed Amelia. "I'm sure it was around the time of the King's Coronation." She thought for a while, "That's right it was – it was just before Carlisle Race Week and Douglas was called over to

Newcastle to sort out a problem there. I remember being very annoyed at our break being disrupted, and when my greenhouse was smashed I felt terribly helpless with him being away."

The King's Coronation; Race week – Armstrong's mind began to race. He turned back to the boy, "Edward, you said a man fell from the bridge when your mummy's greenhouse was broken."

The boy nodded uncertainly, starting to believe he had done something wrong. Cornelius looked to his mother for permission to carry on with his questions. She consented with an uncertain nod of her own.

"Edward, did you see the man fall?"

More silent nodding.

"Can you remember if this was the same day when mummy's greenhouse was broken?"

"Mummy was cleaning the glass."

"Cleaning the glass? Oh you mean cleaning the broken glass? Was this the following day?"

At this, the boy's mother had a sudden recollection, "That's right, I remember now, I was clearing pieces of broken glass out of harm's way when there was another almighty downpour. I rushed back into the house to shelter; Edward was sitting in the front room by the window. I remember him saying something about 'a man' but I was so flustered and concerned with the mess and the rain I didn't pay any attention to it," she lowered her voice slightly, "he often makes random comments and he certainly never said anything about the viaduct."

Armstrong again turned to the youngster, "Edward, was your mummy in the garden when you saw the man?"

"Yes. He fall off the bridge."

"Did you hear him cry out?"

Edward's mother answered the question on her son's behalf, "He can't have done, or I would have heard it. I was out of sight of the viaduct, around the back of the house, but I would have heard a scream."

Surely it couldn't be? The amateur birdwatcher was a policeman once more. "Mrs. Stoneycroft, you must excuse me as I have some important questions to ask the stationmaster Mr. Carter," – his host looked a little bemused, but offered no objection to her guest's curtailed visit – "I can't thank you enough for your hospitality. And you, young Edward," he added, turning to the boy and offering his hand, "I can't thank you enough either." With that, he made his farewells and left the garden via the wooden door and found himself on the riverside track once more.

The Memory of a Good Woman

The last time Inspector Armstrong had interviewed John Carter was two weeks after his brother's death. His first meeting had taken place within days of the tragedy, before the policeman had adopted the fairly standard practice of attending the young man's funeral to see if anything, or anyone, could lead to a new line of enquiry. His attendance however only succeeded in further compounding his frustration. Given Joseph's apparent popularity, Armstrong wondered why there was a relatively low turn-out of mourners, who basically consisted of the deceased's brother, his landlady, and a few colleagues from Brown, Banks & Edwards. All seemed genuinely shocked and upset by Carter's demise, and the policeman concluded any wrongdoing did not lay with the black-clad figures that stood at the graveside as the coffin was lowered.

When Armstrong subsequently interviewed John at length, he learned there were fifteen years between him and his brother, who had the same father but different mothers. He explained that his own mother had died during the delivery of a stillborn infant. John and his father were naturally devastated by the double tragedy; when his father met and married Joseph's mother some years later, it was as though they were a family re-joined.

Because he was considerably older than his brother, John said he found himself very protective of Joseph as he recalled his feelings at losing a younger sibling. This close bond continued into adulthood, and if anything had strengthened still further following their parents' passing.

John had followed in his father's footsteps by embarking on a career on the railway; he had gradually worked his way up from the time of Joseph's birth to his position today of stationmaster at Wetheral.

Joseph, meanwhile, had done well at school and found a position as an apprentice with the firm of solicitors on Castle Street. After ten years he had progressed to the position of personal clerk to David Edwards, one of the partners in the firm.

Having an interest in the world of horse racing, and through some of his employer's circles, Joseph had also found his way to becoming one of the small number of bookmakers' clerks who were employed on a casual basis by the local bookies whenever the races were held in Carlisle. The fact that his death had occurred during the busiest meeting on the calendar was one of the issues that troubled Armstrong. There may have been some connection, but as nothing else seemed amiss during that week in late June 1911, it was difficult to firm the theory up.

Now, nine months on, Cornelius found himself risking opening up the raw wounds on the back of a throw away comment from a young child. *And for what reason? Petty vindication? Personal pride? Would it not just be better to let sleeping dogs lie?*

Whatever the issues wrestling for attention were, he knew his mind wouldn't allow him to dismiss the case without exhausting every possible avenue first – even if that meant upsetting a few people along the way. As he began to retrace his footsteps, he thought of his own personal maxim: *Do the right thing – not the popular thing, or the easy thing – the right thing.*

He climbed the steps back up to the station, crossed the footbridge, and approached the ivy-covered station house where Carter lived with his wife, Bridget. Bracing himself, Cornelius knocked.

The stationmaster opened the door after a few moments, and seemed to take a few moments more to recognise his visitor.

"Hello Mr. Carter," said Cornelius once the stationmaster had placed him.

"Inspector Armstrong, I'm so sorry, I wasn't expecting…"

"Why would you be?" said the policeman with a smile. "It's me who should be apologising for calling on you unannounced, but I wonder if I could talk to you again about Joseph?"

Even though several months had passed since Armstrong had spoken to John outside the Coroners' Court, he noted that the stationmaster still wore the same ashen face, making him seem much older that his forty years. The policeman's comment caused concurrent feelings of shock, hope, sadness, anger and futility within the victim's brother, and after taking some moments to compose himself, Carter stood aside and invited Cornelius inside with a weak smile.

Showing the Inspector through to the kitchen, the stationmaster instinctively checked his pocket watch as part of his regular duties.

"Please don't interrupt your schedule on my account," reassured Armstrong, "if you need to go about your business, its fine; I would just like to ask a few questions that I think may be important."

"I don't have anything now for another twenty minutes," said Carter, indicating a seat at the kitchen table. "Can I get you a cup of tea?"

"No thank you, I've just had a drink," replied Armstrong without elaborating. He knew he had to be as delicate as possible.

"Joseph?" asked his brother, "I thought the matter had been closed?"

"You know my feelings, Mr. Carter. I've recently learned of some new information that may have a bearing on the case.

"Can you remember the day before Joseph's body was found?"

"Yes, I think I told you when we first met; there had been a freak storm a day or two earlier, causing some damage on the Carlisle-Settle line at Cumwhinton. I was asked to go and man the station while the line was repaired."

"So you weren't here for how long?" asked Cornelius, reminding himself.

Carter thought for a while, "It would be the best part of two days, I suppose."

"And Wetheral was left unmanned if memory serves," continued the policeman, referring to their previous interview.

"Yes, that's right."

"Did you have a chance to speak to Joseph before you left?"

"Well, no, there was no reason to. As you're probably aware, Cumwhinton is only a mile away, and I was returning home each night."

"So there was no reason for Joseph to believe you were anywhere other than here?"

"Well, no, I don't suppose so." Carter was struggling to see the point.

"Mr. Carter, can you remember if the river was still swollen at this time?"

"It was, I think. I seem to recall Bridget commenting that she had never seen it so high for so long."

Just then, both men looked up as the latch on the back door clanked open and Carter's wife, Bridget, entered with a basket of fruit and vegetables.

"Oh, I'm sorry," she said as she entered, "John, you never said we were expecting guests."

"It's my fault Mrs. Carter," interrupted Cornelius, "I'm Inspector Armstrong, we met last year."

"Oh yes, of course," said Bridget, remembering Armstrong's last interview with her husband.

"The Inspector was just asking about the height of the river during that storm we had when Joseph…" a lump caught in John's throat as he recalled his brother's death.

His wife rescued her husband's discomfort. "I remember the river *was* high. I don't think I'd ever seen it like that before."

Cornelius's gaze drifted idly from Mrs. Carter to the kitchen window and out into the middle distance and he sat twisting the horns of his moustache.

The Carters exchanged puzzled looks. "Inspector?" John broke the embarrassed silence.

"Oh, I'm sorry," said Armstrong breaking his reverie. "Mr. Carter, I am starting to believe that Joseph came to Wetheral to seek your help shortly before his death.

"I remember you telling me that you were his best friend and confidant. I believe Joseph was in some sort of trouble and came here to see you."

"And unknown to him, I was at Cumwhinton," thought Carter aloud.

"I remember when you were away I was helping the clean-up in the village," added his wife, "so if Joseph did come here, I wouldn't have been here either. I remember now, I should have returned home in the afternoon the second day you were at Cumwhinton, but it bucketed down from lunch-time so I just stayed put at the village hall. I didn't get back much before you."

"Yes, I vaguely recall," said the stationmaster blankly.

"Maybe the box Mr. Edwards gave us might help the Inspector," said Bridget.

Cornelius' blue eyes shot questioningly from one to the other.

Carter sighed with a half-smile, "I forgot all about that."

"What box was this?" asked Armstrong, trying his best to disguise his impatience.

"A couple of months ago," explained John, "Mr. Edwards informed me that a box belonging to Joseph had been found in the basement of his offices."

The questions tumbled through the policeman's mind, "Do you have this box? What was in it? Can I see it?"

A wistful look clouded Carter's face again, "Yes, I have it somewhere. I found it so upsetting I never opened it. I'll see if I can find it."

"I think you put it under the stairs dear," assisted Mrs. Carter.

A few minutes later, the stationmaster returned and placed the small wooden box on the kitchen table. It was of a size that could have contained a pair of shoes, and much to Armstrong's frustration, had a brass fitting on one side. The policeman assumed the box had been delivered to John in the locked state he now found it. He asked about the key with a questioning look.

"To be honest Inspector, I can't remember if Mr. Edwards gave me the key; I'm sure he will have done but I couldn't bring myself to look in the box, so I never paid any attention to it. If I did have a key, I couldn't tell you where I put it."

"Do you mind if I take it away? It could help my investigation tremendously?"

"No, we have no objections," said Carter after giving his wife an affirming glance.

Cornelius thanked the stationmaster and his wife and left the two to their reflections. With his day's bird-watching already forgotten, and believing the case of Joseph Carter's death to be well and truly re-opened, he impatiently waited for the next train to take him back into Carlisle.

The Box

Armstrong's mind raced during the short journey back to the city; he was sorely tempted to smash open the box that sat on his lap, such was his curiosity concerning its contents. But out of reverence to Joseph Carter, and out of respect to his brother John – whose property it now was – he resisted the temptation. Besides, how would it look to his fellow passengers if he suddenly removed his boot and started pounding the damn thing until it shattered into a dozen or more pieces? He gave a half smile to himself at the thought before checking his pocket watch impatiently, and thought about Milo Jones.

The policeman didn't wait for the train to come to a complete standstill – as it decelerated he alighted at a half-run and was virtually exiting the station before his fellow passengers had stepped onto the platform. Within five minutes, Cornelius was hurrying along Globe Lane.

Milo Jones was the best locksmith in the city. His skills at picking locks were legendary and Cornelius had commented on more than one occasion that he believed Jones had taught Harry Houdini all he knew. His favourite story was when Milo was asked by George Moulding, the manager of the National Bank on the corner of English Street and Bank Street, to review the security of the newly installed main safe.

"Good morning Mr. Jones," said Mr. Moulding with a self confident air, "this new safe has been especially commissioned by Head Office for use in all our banks around the country."

"Who fitted the safe, Mr. Moulding?" asked Milo, as he unraveled his battered leather pouch containing an assortment of keys and small picks.

"The manufacturers of the safe itself," replied the bank manager. "It is said to be at the vanguard of security, utilising materials developed by Brinks Incorporated, who became adept at transporting large quantities of gold bullion across the United States."

Milo nodded and smiled politely. "That's nice," he mumbled to himself, "I think you should probably go into the other room now, Mr. Moulding, if you don't mind."

"Why?" asked Moulding a little haughtily.

"Because I don't want you to see what I'm about to do."

The bank manager fingered his collar uncomfortably before acquiescing with a clipped, "Very well."

Moulding walked through into the outer office and went to close the door behind him. "There's no need to close the door Mr. Moulding, you can come back in now," called Milo instantly.

The bank manager stepped back over the threshold to see the locksmith standing beside the open safe – the door gaped wide revealing all the bank's riches. The colour instantly drained from Moulding's face, and his knees threatened to buckle from underneath him. Milo left the poor man being tended to by his secretary who was doing her best to administer tea and sympathy by somehow suggesting things perhaps weren't quite as bad as they appeared.

It was now the turn of another member of Carlisle's officialdom to ask for the locksmith's help.

Milo Jones lived and worked on Globe Lane, one of a series of downtrodden alleyways in the heart of the city. The Lanes consisted of shabby tenements, some of which, like Jones's, doubled as commercial premises. Families lived cheek by jowl in this impoverished enclave that was completely incongruous with the Georgian elegance of Lowther Street at one end, and the business and retail hub of Scotch Street and the market at the other.

Jones's workshop was located halfway along the cobbled lane below his humble living accommodation.

Cornelius Armstrong made his way along the noisy lane that bustled with activity: children played with hoops and tops, while their mothers scrubbed at their front steps and beat the dust from the cork matting that presumably acted as floor covering inside the modest dwellings. All the while, businessmen used the thoroughfare to cut through as they moved between the various business premises in the two main streets at either end of the Lanes.

Cornelius made his way past a wall of barrels, behind which a carter was loading some hessian sacks onto a wagonette. Approaching the locksmith's premises, he gave a frustrated tut when he saw that the door was shut, the usual signal that Milo was not open for business. The doorframe was rotten at its base, and the green paint that once covered the door itself was old and had flaked away in places to reveal the weathered timber beneath. Its condition did not deter Armstrong from standing on ceremony, such was his eagerness to re-ignite his investigations; he banged on the door with the side of his fist.

"MILO!...MILO!"

After almost a minute, the detective heard the sash window on the second floor chafing open. Looking up, he saw the leathery face of Milo Jones appear above him.

"WHAT THE...oh...hello Mr. Armstrong!"

"Hello Milo," called Cornelius, "are you open?"

Knowing it was futile to try and put the policeman off, Jones mumbled to himself, "Bloody looks like it!" as he disappeared from view and slammed the window shut.

After the clanging of a few bolts from the inside, the door creaked open and the proprietor stood to one side to allow Cornelius entry. The policeman got straight to it, "I have this little box Milo, I wonder if you could open it for me?"

The locksmith took the box from him and gave it a cursory look over. Despite the bright day outside, his workshop was dark and dingy. Laying the box on his bench, he lit an oil lamp that succeeded in creating a pool of light across the whole work area.

Holding a watchmaker's loupe up to his eye, his face creased in and out like an accordion until the magnifying lens was held in place in the craftsman's eye socket. Milo then studied the lock of the box in more detail under the light. "Mmm...It's an interesting little thing," he said to himself, and then to his customer, "How precious are you about it?"

"Well it's not mine," said Armstrong, "I'm not particularly interested in the box – it's the contents I'm after. But I'd rather not damage the box – that could cause a bit of upset."

"It could take a little bit of time, could you leave it with me?"

"How long?"

"Half an hour or so."

Cornelius thought of another little errand he could run in the meantime. "That'll be alright," he said, "I'll be back within the half hour."

The errand he thought of was to visit the Registrar's Office and check the deaths that occurred during the last week of June, 1911. With the minimum of fuss, the registrar produced the ledger for the year and sat the Inspector down at a desk in the reception area.

Cornelius felt the adrenalin begin to rush as the turning of the large pages led him towards the information he was looking for...*April... May...June, week commencing 5 June ....week commencing 12 June....Ah, here, week commencing 19 June, 1911.*

He ran his finger down the page; there were six deaths recorded that week: three people in hospital – two of which were a mother and her still-born child – two elderly people died in their respective homes, and Joseph Carter was listed as an 'accidental death.'

If young Edward was right about seeing a man fall from the viaduct, it had to be Joseph – it couldn't be anyone else. "This was no accident," Cornelius said out loud, causing him to feel a little embarrassed as he looked up to see the bemused faces of the staff looking at him. He made his way back to Milo's, convinced more than ever before that Joseph's death was as a result of foul play.

The locksmith had found his way into the box before Cornelius had left Globe Lane, but had spent the stated time making a key for the lock. Upon his arrival, the policeman was impressed once more by the skill of the craftsman – the brass key Jones had fashioned was long, slim and as elegant as the box itself. He paid Milo and hurried back to his lodgings on Abbey Street.

Mrs. Wheeler had decided to take advantage of her lodger's absence by carrying out some spring cleaning. She was in the back yard beating the hall carpet to within an inch of its life when she heard someone coming in the front door. Hurrying back through the kitchen and into the hall, she found Cornelius closing the door behind him.

"*Whadthecawme?* I thought you were away for the day Mr. Armstrong?"

"There was a slight change of plan, Mrs. Wheeler," said Cornelius, as he made towards the stairs, "I found a bit more at Wetheral than I had bargained for. As he climbed the stairs towards his room, he added "A cup of tea would be much appreciated Mrs. Wheeler if you don't mind."

Cornelius couldn't quite make out what Mrs. Wheeler said as he stepped onto the landing and she made her way back toward the kitchen.

The Contents

Cornelius sat at his desk in the sitting room of his lodgings on Abbey Street. As he placed the key in the lock of the box, the thought of those modern-day Egyptologists discovering hitherto unknown artifacts flitted through his mind. Inside, he found a small pile of folded papers. He scooped them up and moved the box to one side.

Spreading the papers out, he found three five pound notes, half a dozen betting slips, a piece of paper ripped from a notebook with a series of initials on it, a single sheet of folded newspaper that had been torn from the *Carlisle Journal*, and a letter addressed to Carter from the Irish Jockey Club. It was these latter three items that intrigued the policeman the most.

First, the newspaper cutting was dated March of the previous year. He unfolded the large sheet and spread it open. On one side, there was a list of deaths and three obituaries filled the rest of the page. On the other, the two main headlines involved local stories about the alterations to Citadel Station that may cause delays, and details of the week's livestock trading at the auction mart. The left hand column of the page was reserved for 'World News'.

Paragraphs included a piece on the 50th anniversary in Russia of the emancipation of 23,000,000 Russian serfs by Tsar Alexander II, details of new governments that were formed in both France and Italy while tragedy struck in the south of the latter country when part of the crater of Mt. Vesuvius fell after a severe earthquake, and a worrying piece on the arms race in Germany where they launched their first turbine powered battleship on the birthday of the late Kaiser Wilhelm I.

Further afield meanwhile, the United States Department of War moved a large body of troops to points in Texas and southern California, amid fears of interference in the affairs of Mexico, and tragedy struck in the southern hemisphere with the sinking of the Australian ship *SS Yongala* in a cyclone, with the loss of 122 passengers and crew.

But Armstrong's attention was drawn to the bottom paragraph that had been circled in pencil. It was a story originating from Dublin:

TRAINER BANNED

> Irish race horse trainer EL Sloon has been banned from racing after being found guilty of race fixing by the Irish Jockey Club. Sloon (full name, Eamon Liam) shot to prominence in 1907 when horses trained by him won some of the biggest races in England, Ireland, and on mainland Europe. Among his many victories was his duel success during Carlisle race week two years ago when In for a Penny won the Carlisle Bells and The Luck of the Irish won the Cumberland Plate. Sloon was found guilty of several offences at the hearing in Dublin, which included tampering with weights to influence the outcome of the race, assisting bookies in laying off bets, and unusual patterns of scratching or removing horses from races immediately prior to the start.

The piece concluded, stating that Sloon had received a five-year ban from racing for his misdemeanors. Just under the paragraph was a picture of the disgraced trainer – a clean-shaven man with short fair hair.

Cornelius sat back in his chair and absentmindedly rubbed the palm of his hand over the top of his closely cropped black hair before tweaking the horns of his mustache. His eyes then rested on the small piece of paper that had seemingly been torn from a notebook, which read:

The Millionaire – CC
Eastern Seaboard – MS
Champagne Charlie – SM
Orlando – CB

In For A Penny – HC
Nickels and Dimes – PS
The Luck of the Irish – KC
Half a Sixpence – DS
d'Artagnan – PM
Amir – AC
Prince's Fare – YO
The Gambler – AS

H.R. Rochester

It was obvious, given Carter's part-time role, that the list related to race horses and presumably their jockeys. But the final entry was strange – *why was that apparently listed separately? And who exactly was HR Rochester?*

He looked at the letter from Dublin. It was a simple acknowledgement which read:

> Dear Mr. Carter,
>
> Thank you for your letter dated 10th October 1909. We will look into the matter in due course.
>
> Yours faithfully,
>
> Declan Murphy
> Secretary of the Jockey Club

Cornelius decided to seek out someone he thought might be of help. He went to rise from his chair when Mrs. Wheeler knocked and entered with a tray on which stood a pot of tea and a plate of toasted teacakes. "I suppose you haven't had anything to eat either," she said, laying the tray on the desk in front of him.

At the smell of the teacakes and the melting butter, the policeman's stomach grumbled in agreement, and Cornelius sank back into his chair, believing it wise and polite to do as he was told, given the inconvenience he had caused his landlady less than twenty minutes earlier.

It was mid-afternoon before he left his lodgings again to take the short walk around the corner to West Walls. But his destination wasn't the Police Station; further down West Walls was the warehouse of fruit merchants WB Anderson – this was Armstrong's destination.

Claude Irwin had been Anderson's warehouse manager for twenty years, and this was the man the policeman was keen to talk to. Claude was a slightly built man with a high forehead and wispy red hair in his late fifties; he was coming to the end of his working day having met the northbound early-morning train at the station, from where he supervised the distribution of fruit and veg to Anderson's various outlets in West Cumberland and South West Scotland. He was alone in the warehouse, checking the crates, barrows and boxes that would be used to carry out the same tasks the following morning, when he looked up and saw the policeman walking through the gaping entrance to the warehouse.

"Hello Mr. Armstrong, what can I do for you? I'm just about to lock up for the day."

"Hello Claude, before you go, I wonder if I could trouble you with a few more racing questions."

Like Joseph Carter, the warehouse manager worked as a part time bookies' clerk when there were race meetings held at the Blackwell Road course. He therefore knew Carter reasonably well but like many others, when questioned by the policeman after the young man's death the previous year, Claude couldn't offer any plausible explanation for the tragic event.

Armstrong took the newspaper cutting and the piece of note paper from his pocket and showed them to Irwin. "I think these belonged to Joseph Carter," he said. "Do you know why he would have them and what they mean?"

Claude took his glasses out of the top pocket of his brown dust coat and put them on. "Well that's certainly the young lad's hand," he said, referring to the hand-written page, "we all used to rib him about how neat his writing was."

"I assume those are names of horses and their riders?" asked Armstrong, pointing to the page, "do you see any significance in the names?"

Irwin studied them for a while. "The obvious one for me is In for a Penny. Irish Horse – could run like the clappers! It won the Cumberland Plate two or three years ago – long odds an' all if memory serves. I think that Luck of the Irish won the Bells as well." He looked again at the list, "Half a Sixpence was a Derby-winner. Not sure about the others," he said, handing the paper back to the Inspector.

"What about the newspaper?" questioned Armstrong, motioning Irwin to study the page, "The lad seems to have circled the story about the Irish trainer."

"Oh yes, old Sloony! I remember him. A real Irish rogue if ever there was one. He certainly got his comeuppance didn't he? Skedaddled to America the last I heard. If I'm not mistaken, those two horses that won in Carlisle were his – I think the Derby winner was too come to think of it."

"Did you ever see this Sloon?"

"Yes, he would travel all over the place with his horses – seen him in Carlisle a few times. That's him alright," he added, pointing to the picture in the newspaper, "you obviously can't see it on there but he had a decent head of ginger hair. Happy days!" he said with a smile, rubbing his own receding locks.

"Do you know if Carter would have had anything to do with him?" asked Armstrong, keen to return to the subject at hand.

"Not especially," said Claude thoughtfully, "but come to think of it I seem to remember the young lad having words with his bookie Silas Baxter once over. I was only on the edge of it, and I couldn't hear much for the din of the crowd, but I'm sure Sloon's name was mentioned at one point." Irwin removed his dust coat and hung it on the back of the office door. "If you leave it with me Mr. Armstrong, I'll see if I can remember anything else, and I'll nip round and see you sometime."

"Thank you Claude, I would really appreciate that. One more thing, isn't there a meeting on at the moment?"

"There is," replied Irwin, "The Spring Meeting – I'll be working up there tomorrow afternoon myself."

Armstrong helped the warehouse manager lever the large sliding doors shut with a bang. "Thanks again Claude," he said, "I think I will be, too."

The Spring Meeting 1909

The conversation Claude Irwin was trying to recall took place during Carlisle's Spring Meeting three years earlier.

At the end of the second day of the three-day meeting, Joseph Carter was tidying up the takings and paperwork of his bookie, Silas Baxter. When marking up the ledger, he noticed an unusually large amount of money set against a horse called Champagne Charlie that was due to be running in the big race the following day. His bookie had to leave early "…on urgent business," so Joseph didn't have a chance to bring it to his attention.

The strange entries continued to trouble the young man as he took a tram back to his lodgings on London Road: *why would so much be laid against an unknown horse in a fairly modest early-season race in Carlisle? And what was so special about Champagne Charlie, anyway?* Questions that puzzled Joseph prompted him to wade through the pile of monthly racing periodicals he had collected from the time he first became seriously interested in racing.

The only reference he could find to the horse was in the June 1908 edition of the *Racing Times* – it carried a story about Irish trainer E.L. Sloon and the latest additions to his already talented stable. It appeared to Carter that the horse had never actually raced, and if that *were* the case, then the following day would be the horse's debut; and if *that* were the case, then someone, somewhere, had some inside information.

The following day, Joseph made sure that he was at the track early as he wanted to see the horse in question before the working day began. It was a little before eight o'clock as he stood at the side of the track near the finishing post. In the far distance, a silhouetted line of horses and riders emerged through the early-morning mist. Further down the track, about a hundred yards from where Carter was standing, he recognised the figure of E.L. Sloon, trainer of the horse. He was with another larger man Joseph didn't recognise.

As the line of horses approached, the lead rider eased his mount across the track towards the two men – the others carried on past Carter towards the paddock area. The young man looked at the remaining horse down the track: it was a beautiful large chestnut with four white stockings. Its jockey was leaning down over its neck and appeared to be engaging in animated conversation with the two men who stood below him. Finally, the three appeared to agree on whatever they were discussing; Sloon and his companion turned and walked back towards the deserted officials' area, while the jockey encouraged his horse forward in the direction of where Carter stood.

"Is this Champagne Charlie?" asked the young man as it walked by.

"It certainly is." The jockey's thick Irish accent couldn't disguise his pride in his handsome mount; he gave it a loving slap and rub on the neck.

"It should do well this afternoon?" ventured the bookie's clerk.

The jockey seemed to snap out of his affectionate trance and looked at Carter for the first time. He didn't answer, and simply kept his horse moving.

Throughout the rest of the day, Joseph tried to raise the matter with his bookie Silas Baxter, but was continually ignored or diverted into doing something else by his employer.

As the crowds grew, the atmosphere built and the noise intensified. Joseph Carter was increasingly looking forward to the last race of the day, when he would see the horse that he had become so interested in. But instead of answering the questions swilling around in Carter's mind, the race was to only succeed in prompting even more.

He watched through his binoculars as the starter's flags descended on the far side of the course. Champagne Charlie led in the early stages, but as the field rounded the final corner, the Irish horse appeared to labour and the grey Wild Orchid eased past with three furlongs to go. The customary roar went up from the grandstand as the field thundered for home, and Carter watched with some bewilderment as Champagne Charlie tailed off badly. Through the clods of earth thrown up by the ten-strong field, Joseph saw the jockey sit up on the line and found himself pipped for fifth place.

Amid the usual comingled groans and cheers, Carter dashed over to the unsaddling enclosure. Champagne Charlie approached, snorting and shaking its head, almost appalled by its own performance, and steam rose from the flanks of the horse as the blanket was draped over him. A few people milled around but there was no sign of the trainer, Sloon.

Carter half expected a steward's enquiry, such was the lethargy shown by the magnificent animal; he even wondered if they had actually called Sloon to the steward's room to explain his horse's performance – why else would the trainer be absent from such a scene? He noted the matter-of-fact body language of the jockey which was very different from the bullish appearance of the rider Carter had witnessed that same morning. Very little was said between the jockey and the few people who were present, and the stable lad simply gave the horse a pat on the neck before walking him away. The small group of people then dispersed shortly afterwards in different directions.

No announcement, no enquiry, no Sloon. How odd. Carter wandered back over to Baxter's stand.

"'Ere! Where have you been?" cried the bookie, as he tried to attend to several customers at once.

"I went over to see that Champagne Charlie – he's trained by the Irish chap, Sloon."

"Never mind that," interrupted Baxter, "you'll be making a right bloody Charlie of us both if you don't sort this lot out." He gesticulated towards the crowd of customers who were tying up their own business at the end of the day's racing.

After what Carter believed was an unusual sequence of events at that Spring Meeting, the young man kept an eye on the racing press in order to chart the progress of the Irish horse. He noted with some interest that it won the Newmarket Stakes later in the season by ten lengths.

By this time, another horse had come to the attention of the young clerk. Orlando was a horse from the same stable as Champagne Charlie, and was heavily tipped to run well in the Carlisle Bells in the same year.

Carter noticed the same pattern: lots of money placed on the horse days in advance only for it to disappoint in the race itself. Given that Sloon was also the trainer, and the horse romped home in the St Leger that September, Carter became suspicious that something funny was going on with Sloon's horses. As the season went on, interest and curiosity led to eagerness, which in turn led to an obsession with the Irish stable of E. L. Sloon.

During those spring and summer months of 1909, young Carter studied the racing press for patterns and comments. He then went through his back issues of the *Racing Times*. He discovered that – over a three year period – on no less than five occasions, highly-fancied horses trained by Sloon were scratched shortly before their races, while it seems another four were criticized for underperformance before delivering big wins in prestigious races later in the season.

More alarmingly, the pattern was not only restricted to England. Two instances occurred each in France and America, while Carter found evidence of at least one race in both Ireland and even Australia.

He calculated that Sloon's horses had taken part in over fifty races in the one calendar year. If he had rigged as little as five or even ten, then the chances of him being found out would be extremely remote. Furthermore, if those five or ten were scattered around the world, with just one or two questionable races taking place in each country, they would be so few and so infrequent that they would barely raise any suspicion.

Throughout the 1909 season, when Carter tried to raise his concerns with Baxter – who continually changed the subject every time it was brought up – it fleetingly crossed his mind that his part-time employer might know something more than he was letting on.

By the end of the season, he resolved to write to the Irish Jockey Club to report his suspicions. Despite the fact that he received an acknowledgement, no word was forthcoming as the 1910 season began. That did not dissuade Carter however, and as race week approached, he was absolutely certain there was clear evidence of wrongdoing in relation to Sloon's horses across the previous three seasons in at least five different countries. Any chance of gathering further evidence was negated however when – a fortnight before the meeting – Sloon withdrew the three horses he was due to bring to Carlisle. The questions now facing the young man were how could he prove any corruption, and who would listen to him even if he did?

The Spring Meeting 1912

The Spring Meeting was firmly established as the second most important meeting of Carlisle's racing year, behind the prestigious Bells and Plate Meeting which was the very reason for race week itself, when the whole city would shut down.

Three years on from Joseph Carter's suspicions, Cornelius Armstrong followed the thousands of race-goers on the specially arranged trams and omnibuses that took them from the centre of the city on the four-mile journey up Blackwell Road to the course at the far south-east outskirts of Carlisle. He was going there, not so much to watch the horses, but to watch the watchers, to see if anything could explain the strange scribblings of Carter, to see if Claude Irwin could remember anything further since their chat yesterday, and above all else, to see the young man's bookie, Silas Baxter.

The day was in keeping with the previous morning, when Cornelius had intended to enjoy a gentle day's bird watching at Wetheral – young Edward Stoneycroft, John and Bridget Carter, Milo Jones, and then Claude Irwin had all put a stop to that. Armstrong was once again the inquisitive policeman; with all of his instincts telling him there was much wrongdoing. Furthermore, he was convinced the racecourse could provide him with answers to many of his questions.

As the crowd roared at the sight of the horses on the home straight during the first race, Cornelius tried to position himself on the raised terracing at the foot of the grandstand. The futility of trying to distinguish anyone from the sea of waving arms and hats prompted the policeman to try a different tack.

He moved towards the paddock area that included the parade ring and the winners' enclosure. The winner of the first race was announced as "...Twenty Bucks, trained by Solomon Neal." Polite applause rippled round the enclosure as the horse was led in. The stable lad draped a blanket over the hind quarters as the jockey slid off its back to be greeted by a rotund man with shoulder length black hair and a thick beard – *presumably the owner?* thought Armstrong. Beside him was a big man who appeared more interested in keeping people away from the man and his horse.

Armstrong left them to it and picked his way through the crowd to the row of bookies' stands that were set back from the home straight. The Inspector scoured the line of around a dozen bookies; they were all perched on top of their wooden steps waving, shouting, and tick tacking down the line above the din of the excited crowd. Each had a sign with their name attached to their respective stands. The strange thing was that Silas Baxter wasn't there.

"*Mr. Armstrong, sir!*" shouted a voice along the line.

Cornelius looked along and saw Claude Irwin; he was standing at the foot of the stand marked 'Jimmy Brisco', waving at the policeman.

"Hello Claude," he said as he passed some happy customers who were presumably collecting on the first race, "I didn't see you there. I was looking for Silas Baxter but he doesn't seem to be here?"

"No that's right – I noticed that myself when we were setting up this morning. Not like him I must say." Claude saw the frustration in the policeman's face. "We are blessed with racing royalty mind you – that trainer of the first winner."

"Was that the bloke with the beard?" asked Armstrong.

"Yeah, that's him. Big Yank – been cleaning up all over the place for the past couple of years. Nobody can touch him. Don't know what he's doing here mind – must be slumming it!"

"Who was the bloke with him?"

"Probably his henchman. When I say no one can get near him, I'm not just talking about his horses on the track!" Claude then snapped his fingers in realisation, "I do have something for you though Mr. Armstrong." He reached down behind the stand and brought out a large bag of what looked like periodicals. "These are all of my back copies of the

Racing Times, going back five years. They're pretty heavy," he gasped as he heaved them across, "but they might help you find a pattern or whatever you are looking for – keep them as long as you like."

With that, he was pulled back to his regular duties by a throng of customers waving their betting slips at him.

"Thanks for the books Claude!" called Cornelius as he turned to go. As he did so, he came face to face with another acquaintance of his. "Reuben!"

"*Uh*! Oh, er, hello Mr. Armstrong."

Reuben Hanks was the archetypal lovable rogue; growing up in the same downtrodden area of the city as Cornelius, the two had known each other for most of their lives. Whereas Armstrong had bettered himself to the point of becoming a senior police officer, Hanks had spent most of his life ducking and diving from one sticky situation to the next. It was probably fair to say that Reuben had not *exactly* fallen onto the wrong side of the tracks, but it was an equally fair observation to suggest he spent most of his time balancing on the tracks themselves.

Cornelius had been proved correct over the years in believing that it was better to utilise Reuben's skills as an informant rather than to waste his time trying to uncover the various scams that Hanks would undoubtedly be involved in. The two therefore enjoyed a mutual understanding that ultimately benefitted them both.

"I've been thinking about getting in touch," said the Inspector, who was not that surprised to see Reuben at the races; nor was he surprised to see him winning.

For his part, Hanks always liked to keep their relationship as discrete as possible. In this case, that meant not being seen talking to the policeman when his associates were close by. "I'll just collect me winnings Mr. Armstrong and I'll meet you behind the grandstand in five minutes."

Sure enough, a few minutes later, the ragtag figure of Reuben Hanks – having checked several times that no one was watching him – appeared in the shadows where the policeman waited.

"Reuben, what do you know about Silas Baxter?"

"The bookie? He's alright I suppose – bit of a sniveling la'al bugger. What's he been up to?"

"I'm not sure to be honest. He used to have a young clerk who worked for him; he was found dead last year – supposedly accidentally."

"You think Baxter done him in?" asked Reuben, and then offered an answer himself, "I don't think he would be up to that."

"No, not necessarily. It's just I think the boy was on to some sort of race fiddling and was hoping that Baxter could fill in a few gaps. I spoke to him last year but I've come by some new information that I would like to ask him about. It relates to the Irish trainer, Sloon."

"The bloke that was banned? Aye he was a right wrong 'un."

Armstrong did his best to suppress a smile as the words 'kettle' and 'black' flitted through his mind.

"Did you ever see him?"

"Saw him up here a few times, that's all. He had a bloke who looked after him, called McAllindon – he disappeared an' all not long after Sloon left the scene."

Armstrong took a small notebook from his inside pocket and wrote down the name. He then remembered the 'henchman', as Irwin called him, in the winners' enclosure with Neal. "Like the bloke with the American?" he asked.

"Yeah. His name is Dawson, he comes in 'Blue Lugs' on a night. Apparently he is staying with some auntie of his who lives in Caldewgate."

Cornelius made a note of his name too, and saw an opportunity for Hanks to do some investigation work on his behalf. He reached into his trouser pocket this time and pulled out some coins and pressed three giuneas into the palm of Hanks's hand with his thumb. The informant's eyes lit up at the sight. "Reuben, if you see Dawson in 'Blue Lugs' tonight, I want you to make him feel very welcome, if you know what I mean. I want to know anything you can find out about this American, Neal. And see if you can see if there is a connection between him and Silas Baxter."

"Stone me, Mr. Armstrong!" exploded Hanks, and then – remembering the need for discretion – in a lowered voice, "you really are serious about wanting information!"

Cornelius's pride was heavily dented by what he felt was his failure with the original investigation concerning Joseph Carter's death; now he felt he had a second chance to clear the matter up and he was determined to take it. "I am, Reuben," he said, "I am."

Reuben's Stage

The Joiners' Arms stood on the corner of Bridge Street and Byron Street in the heart of Caldewgate, the Irish quarter of the city. The pub was run by Ernie Jeffers, although very few of his clientele appeared to be familiar with his given name. Ernie was known to enjoy a drink himself (in fact, many believed he was never destined to turn a profit from his establishment because of his enthusiasm for this pastime) and the comical result of this was that, over the years, his oversized ears gradually turned a distinct shade of indigo. This gave him and his establishment the inevitable nickname of 'Blue Lugs.'

His pub was a typical working class establishment: stone floors, trestle tables and wooden benches. Most nights saw a packed house of navvies, railway workers and labourers drinking, smoking, and eventually singing their way towards kicking-out time.

This night was no exception: Reuben Hanks had been given his orders by Inspector Armstrong and was there with his companions, waiting for the man who may be able to help Armstrong with his case; and if anything could help Armstrong, that same thing could indirectly help Reuben.

The man in question was Michael Dawson from Kildare, near Dublin. He had landed a job guarding the well-being of American race-horse trainer Solomon Neal. Dawson had been to Carlisle on three previous occasions, and had stayed with an elderly aunt in Poet's Corner, just at the back of Blue Lugs. Her parents had arrived in the city in the latter half of the nineteenth century along with thousands of other Irish immigrants.

Whenever Dawson visited his aunt, it was natural for him to frequent Blue Lugs on an evening and, with Neal tucked up safely in his lodgings elsewhere in the city, tonight was no different. In his late thirties, he was a fit man of about five feet ten, brown hair, and a dark complexion.

In the smoky, raucous pub, Reuben was positioned with his back to the wall where he could see the door; with him was his faithful little black pug Athos, who sat quietly under his master's seat, and his usual associates, most of whom lived within staggering distance of their favourite hostelry.

Barnie Edwards went by the derogatory nickname of 'Bog Rat'. Even in the rough working class environment of Caldewgate, Bog Rat Barnie took great delight in appalling even *his* contemporaries. His habits – which *he* found highly amusing – included cutting the fat off a strip of bacon and pushing it up his nose when no one was looking. A few minutes later, he would then make an exaggerated motion of exploring the orifice with his index finger, and once he was satisfied everyone was looking on with wide-eyed curiosity and disgust, he would gradually pull the six-inch strip out and swallow it whole, much to the jeering horror of his unsuspecting audience.

Jimmy Elliot worked as a navvy alongside Barnie and lived in Wapping over a mile away. He liked Blue Lugs "…coz-a-the-craik and it gives me a chance to sober up on the way home to the missus!" Bobby Lloyd, or 'Lloydy' to one and all, was a wise-cracking Liverpudlean who had come to the city with the railway. Now, he worked as a lamplighter in and around the centre of the city. It was Lloydy who would rib another of the group, Frankie Notman, mercilessly about his stammer. This would have the inevitable effect of worsening the poor man's impediment, as he became excited and frustrated in equal measure, whilst struggling to verbally respond to the deliberately provocative abuse.

The group of drinking pals were made up of Danny McKay, a young man who enjoyed the company but remained largely silent alongside his raucous friends, and Willie Tyson who sported a thick head of blond hair and a matching beard. When William Fredrick Cody's Wild West Show had toured Britain in 1904, and came to Carlisle in September of that year, everyone went down to Bitts Park to see the event. The sharp witted Lloydy thereafter christened Tyson 'Buffalo Bill', which was quickly shortened to 'Buff'.

So the stage was set for Reuben, all he needed now was for Dawson to show up – he wasn't to be disappointed. Shortly before eight o'clock – and immediately after Bog Rat had eased himself off the wooden bench to break wind violently, causing his drinking pals to sound a collective *"WHOA!!!"* – the visitor entered the pub that was already filled with an alcohol-scented mist.

Hanks wasted no time in making for the bar where the Irishman was ordering a drink. "How ye doin'?" he said, making general conversation.

"Grand," said Dawson in his soft accent.

"Are you on your own tonight?" asked Reuben, knowing full well that he was.

"That I am, I'm just here for the racing."

"Oh that's right," said the local, feigning surprise, "I think I saw you at the races this afternoon." Before Dawson could respond, Hanks added, "d'ye fancy joining me and the lads?" indicating the table that was still in a state of some upset following Bog Rat's contribution to the evening's entertainment.

"Whadya want?" Bog Rat was asking his colleagues, "O-di-colone?"

"Aye that's very kind of you," said Dawson to Hanks.

As Reuben stood aside to allow his guest past, he slipped two of Armstrong's guineas into Blue Lugs's hand, "Keep the ale flowing," he whispered, much to the barman's delight.

Reuben's introductions to his colleagues coincided with a call from across the room, "C'mon Stan, give us a tune!" An old boy by the fire reached under the table and produced a squeeze box; the table he was sitting at instantaneously broke out into *Roll Out The Barrel*.

Back at Reuben's table, he started his interrogation.

"So what brings you here then?"

"My auntie just lives round the corner. Whenever I'm in Carlisle I always stay with her."

"How often is that then?"

"Oh, now and then. I've been a few times on my own, but I'm here today with my boss."

Just then, the publican's wife, Audrey, came over to the table with a jug of ale. Barnie Edwards smiled stupidly at her. "Hello Audrey love," he said through his heavy-lidded stupor.

The publican's wife clearly read his intentions, "Get out of it, ye stinking pig!"

"I think your charms are working there, Barnie lad," said Lloydy, much to the amusement of Jimmy and Buff.

Above the din of the laughter and music, Hanks filled up Dawson's tankard and resumed his questioning, knowing he had to be a little subtle in his approach. "Are you with one of the Irish trainers then?"

"No, he's an American." Dawson appeared to inwardly rebuke himself but then relaxed, believing his indiscretion could have no significant consequences.

And so the game continued: the barman's wife continued to supply a seemingly endless supply of ale, whilst avoiding Bog Rat's clumsy advances; the singing and laughter continued throughout, and all the while Reuben asked Michael Dawson questions about his racing connections, whilst continually topping up his tankard from the slopping jug on the table in front of them.

By the end of the evening, he had discovered that Dawson had not met Solomon Neal and didn't know anything about horse racing, prior to his employment. Where was Neal staying? With a bookie friend of his – Silas somebody-or-other. How often did he come to Carlisle? This was his first time. Where were they going next? Dawson was going back to Ireland, but Neal had urgent business in America.

The tired singing signaled an end to the boisterous night. Reuben's friends were the last to leave; Athos appeared to know it was home time as he came out from under the bench, just as his master helped Dawson onto the street. The fresh air came as a shock. "I think I'll be alright now," mumbled Dawson.

"Are you sure," asked Hanks, "I can help you back to your digs if you like?"

"No, no…I'll be fine." Dawson let go of Reuben and swayed until he controlled his balance sufficiently to start the precarious journey home.

Hanks stood under a gas light and watched the Irishman who resembled a dressage horse diagonally crossing its legs in a forward motion. As he zigzagged out of sight Reuben contemplated his findings. He resolved to visit Armstrong the following day. As he himself prepared to leave, he heard the distinctive closing-time sound in the alley to the side of Blue Lugs. Looking round the corner of the lane he saw Bog Rat leaning on the wall and urinating into the gutter. Struggling to remain upright he was mumbling to himself, "ee, what a great night."

"How you getting on, Barnie?" asked Hanks.

"Hey, hey – Reuben, me old pal!" Edwards looked up with an imbecilic grin, "ee, yer a grand lad. I'm just having a Jimmy Riddle!"

"Yeah, so I see." Once he'd finished, Reuben said, "Come on, let's get you home." He hitched Bog Rat's arm over his own shoulder, and proceeded down Byron Street while trying to keep his head away from the stench of his companion. Athos silently followed, having witnessed the scene on many an occasion.

Looking at the strange four-legged silhouette as it faded into the distance, Bog Rat could be heard breathing into Reuben's face, "I don't think that Audrey's my type anyway…"

Down Boundary

The bottom of Blackwell Road meets four other streets and is known colloquially as 'the Boundary', a term derived from the changes to the city perimeters by the Carlisle Corporation Act of 1887. From the Boundary, you would take an omnibus over St Nicholas' Bridge up Botchergate and back into the centre of the city.

But after the races the previous day, Cornelius Armstrong decided to get off the omnibus at the Boundary; his reason being to seek out Silas Baxter, who's betting shop was located there, among the pocket of local shops and facilities around the junction of the five roads. Much to Armstrong's frustration, no amount of banging on the front door of the shop attracted any response from the unlit interior. He trudged over the bridge back into the city, pondering the day's events, and wondered if Reuben Hanks might have more luck in his unorthodox enquiries.

The next day, he sent a telegram to Doctor James Bell, notifying him that he would call to see him at his home in Eden Town, Stanwix, later that afternoon. The morning however would be given over to visiting Joseph Carter's former employer David Edwards to see if he could shine any light of the contents of Carter's wooden box, given that it was Edwards who gave it to the deceased's brother John some months earlier.

"I do remember giving Mr. Cater the box, Inspector," said Edwards after welcoming him into his office, "but I wasn't aware of the contents. It was young Jenny who gave it to me."

Armstrong looked questioningly at the solicitor, not being aware of anyone called Jenny.

Responding to the silent prompt, Edwards continued, "Jenny Little was our office junior at the time of Joseph's death. She's been with us for two years now and is progressing well. We hope to make her our first female clerk this year – it's a modern world out there, Inspector."

"I don't understand what this has to do with Carter," said Cornelius, a little frustrated by Edwards's tangents.

"Well, the two got on very well together and my understanding is that Miss Little and Mr. Carter were – how does one put it – seeing each other in a social capacity."

Armstrong was even more puzzled by this revelation. He had questioned most of the staff at Brown, Banks & Edwards – who had nothing tangible to offer by way of an explanation for the young man's demise – during the original investigation. Before he could voice this, Edwards continued.

"As you might imagine, Miss Little was terribly upset by the whole affair, and requested a month's leave of absence to stay with her family in Kirkby Stephen."

The policeman – angry at his overseeing the fact that Carter may have had a sweetheart, and even angrier that no one felt it appropriate to tell him – exhaled loudly through the nose.

"I can ask her to come in if that would help," said the solicitor, by way of assuaging the Inspector's mood.

"If you wouldn't mind," said Armstrong evenly.

A few minutes later, a pretty young woman with blond hair tied in a bun entered and was introduced the Inspector, who took out his notebook and pencil as a matter of course. After a few preliminary questions, Cornelius turned to the subject of the box.

"Miss Little, can you remember when Joseph gave you the box?"

"It wasn't long before…" she paused, realising what she was about to say.

Her employer poured her a glass of water as she sniveled into a handkerchief, "Take your time, Jenny, there is no rush."

Composed once more, the young woman resumed her tale, "It wasn't long before he died, Inspector. He asked me to look after it for him."

"Why did he give it to you? Did he seem agitated in any way?"

"Yes, he did, Inspector. I think he tried to disguise it for my sake, but a woman's intuition told me that all was not well. That is why I couldn't cope when the dreadful news came and I had to go home to my parents' house to recuperate."

"Do you remember him mentioning anyone's name during this period that might make you to believe they were the cause of Joseph's discomfort?"

"I questioned Joseph several times on the subject and I do remember him mentioning some Scotchman – Mc...McLi...I can't remember exactly."

Armstrong looked at the adjacent page in his notebook to the one he was writing on. It contained the information he had scribbled down the previous day. "Not McAllindon, by any chance?" he asked, looking up.

"Yes, yes, that was it – McAllindon. I remember Joseph saying he was a dangerous man, but he wouldn't elaborate on this, and when I asked him what connection he had with him, he simply changed the subject."

Cornelius thanked the young woman and her employer and left them, believing he had a promising new line of enquiry. He made the short journey back to Abbey Street to pick up some papers. Entering his lodgings, he heard the familiar voice of Mrs. Wheeler from the back kitchen.

"Mr. Armstrong! Is that you, Mr. Armstrong?"

He went through to find his landlady and her daughter Emma folding some bed-sheets that had just been ironed. "Come here lass," said Emma's mother, snatching the sheet from her, "you're like a flea at a wedding! Ah, Mr. Armstrong, that queer looking fella was here earlier looking for you."

"Reuben?"

"Aye, he's got a face that would frighten the bairns – said he would call back tomorrow night."

"Thank you, Mrs. Wheeler," said Cornelius, chuckling to himself on his way back into the hallway and towards the stairs.

After a bite to eat, the policeman embarked on his second appointment of the day – that of visiting the pathologist, Doctor Bell. He wanted to share his recent findings with Bell and ask if he thought it possible for the body to float down the river from Wetheral to the Eden Bridges and sustain the injuries it did.

Upon being shown into the drawing room of the town house in Eden Town, Cornelius was surprised to see that the Doctor already had a visitor – a man in uniform sat on the opposite side of the fire from his host. Both men rose as the policeman was shown in.

"Ah, Cornelius, let me introduce my cousin *Joseph* Bell."

Armstrong could see the family resemblance and offered a hand, "I'm sorry, I didn't realise you had company; I can come back later if it is inconvenient."

"Not at all," said James. "Joseph's just making a hasty visit to Carlisle before embarking on his latest adventure." His cousin picked up the story.

"Nice to meet you Inspector. I work for the White Star shipping company."

"Chief Engineer no less," interrupted his cousin with pride. "The family were farmers, Inspector, near Brampton, but Joseph here had other ideas and served his time as an engine fitter. When did you join the White Star, Joseph?"

"1885 – a few years ago now," replied the cousin with a smile.

"Just come off the *Olympic,*" resumed the Doctor, "to be transferred to the *Titanic!*"

Armstrong looked slightly embarrassed at the two cousins – they obviously thought that he should know a bit about the vessels that Bell was referring to. To spare the policeman's blushes any longer, the Chief Engineer took a leaflet from his inside pocket and handed it over. It described how the vessel had been built at the Harland and Wolff Shipyard in Belfast, along with its sister Olympic ship. '*First Class passengers are arriving from all over the world to experience the trans-Atlantic voyage in the lap of luxury. Among their number are the following VIPs:*

Colonel John Astor, New York City, NY – Property Developer
Mr. Mauriz Hakan Bjornstrom-Steffansson, Stockholm, Sweden – Businessman

Mr Paul Romaine Marie Léonce Chevré, Paris, France - Sculptor
Dr Washington Dodge, San Francisco, California – Politician
Colonel Archibald Gracie IV, Washington DC – Writer
Mr Hyman Rothstein, Rochester, NY – Businessman
Mr Joseph Bruce Ismay, Liverpool, England – Ship owner
Mr Colonel (Oberst) Alfons Simonius-Blumer, Basel, Switzerland – Banker
Mr Benjamin Guggenheim, Philadelphia, Pennsylvania - Businessman'

"She makes her maiden voyage in two weeks' time," said the engineer, "I'm just saying my goodbyes before joining her in Belfast for her sea trials on Sunday."

"That's really impressive," said Cornelius.

"Yes, we're all proud of our Joseph," said the Doctor.

"You've not done badly yourself," said the Chief Engineer to his cousin.

Turning to the reason for his visit, Armstrong took the sailor's lead, "Yes, if you don't mind James, I'd like to ask your opinion on some recent findings regarding the Carter case."

"Are you still pursuing that, Cornelius?" asked Bell with some surprise.

"It's not just blind pride and stubbornness that's leading me on, I assure you," replied the policeman. He proceeded to tell the pathologist about the events of the previous few days and his strengthening belief that the man young Edward Stoneycroft saw fall from the Wetheral Viaduct was Carter. "Do you think the injuries you saw would be conducive with such a sequence of events?" he asked finally.

"Well I suppose they could," said the Doctor. "The head injuries could have been caused before he entered the water or by the fact that the body crashed into the pier at the base of the arches. One thing is for sure – regardless of the head injuries – there was no question that he was dead before he fell or was thrown into the river."

"Thank you, James," said Cornelius, shaking his hand, "that is extremely helpful. And you, Joseph," he added, turning to his cousin, "let me wish you good luck and a safe trip."

The Investigation Heads North

On a dreich morning in early April 1912, Detective Inspector Cornelius Armstrong found himself standing beside the Monkland Canal in Scotland's second city looking up at the imposing Barlinnie Prison. The gaol was capable of holding up to 200 inmates – considerably bigger than the County Gaol in Carlisle – but Armstrong was interested in just one.

The strange sequence of events that had led him to this place had taken place the previous day and had unfolded very quickly.

After receiving his new line of enquiry from young Jenny Little, Armstrong wasted little time in contacting a colleague of his who he hoped might know a little more background – or even the whereabouts – of the men he was looking for.

Detective Inspector Robert Mather was based in Manchester and had taken to collecting a scrapbook of villains, who – once they had made their way into his leger – he subsequently tracked around the country. As a consequence of Mather's diligence, he found that the close fraternity of Detective Inspectors invariably approached him about their latest quarry.

Cornelius had heard about Mather from their mutual friend Inspector Daniel Standish from Preston, but had never had cause to contact the Manchester policeman. That all changed when Armstrong contacted Mather by telephone and asked him about Seamus McAllindon and H.R. Rochester.

"McAllindon?" said Mather – Armstrong could almost picture him smiling at the other end of the telephone, "Oh yes, I know dear old Seamus – he's one of my regulars! I've followed his progress all over the country for many a year. Used to be tangled up in race horse fiddles if memory serves. Had something to do with that Irish fella…" he paused, seemingly racking his brain.

"E.L. Sloon?" helped Armstrong.

"Yes, that's him, Sloon. Disappeared for a while after Sloon was disqualified, but sure enough he turned up recently, brawling and making a nuisance of himself in Glasgow. According to my records he is locked up there at the moment doing a short spell in Barlinnie Gaol."

Armstrong's mind was racing with excitement, "And Rochester?" he ventured.

"Never heard of him now," said Mather, intrigued.

"I don't have any information about him I'm afraid," explained Cornelius, "but I came across his name in connection with Sloon and one or two others apparently involved in racing. There is also an American who's shown up over here recently called Solomon Neal; again, Rochester might be something to do with him but I can't be sure."

Mather thought for a while, "I know a detective in New York. I could wire him if you like, and see if he knows anything of Rochester or Neal."

Cornelius couldn't thank the Manchester man enough, and as soon as the telephone connection went dead, he immediately asked the operator to connect him with Barlinnie Gaol in Glasgow. A brief conversation with Governor Stuart Fraser followed; Fraser confirmed McAllindon was in his custody and gave the policeman permission to visit the gaol the following day. A three-hour train journey and a hansom cab ride from Central Station later, and Cornelius now found himself looking up at the black-bricked monolithic structure, wondering if he was now on the brink of solving the strange death of Joseph Carter, a hundred miles south of here eight months earlier.

The day was cold, and the slate-grey skies deposited a fine drizzle that made the cobblestones beneath Armstrong's feet glisten. The clouds of smut from Glasgow's factory chimneys covered everything like a shroud and succeeded in blackening the buildings, giving the whole city a dark, menacing appearance.

Armstrong was admitted into the prison, and despite his visiting the County Gaol back home on many occasions, the dark, threatening environment never ceased to have an effect on him. Barlinnie of course, was bigger – much bigger, and was therefore far more intimidating than its counterpart in Carlisle. This gave the hollow building an even more intimidating atmosphere.

The Inspector was shown along seemingly endless corridors, protected at each end by large iron gates that gave off a loud echoing clang every time the prison guard closed them behind him and his visitor. Finally, Armstrong was escorted to an open iron stairway that led to what turned out to be the Governor's Office.

Governor Stuart Fraser was an unusually young man given his status – barely forty, estimated Cornelius. He greeted the policeman cordially, "Welcome, Inspector Armstrong, this must be a serious matter indeed to bring you north of the border at such short notice."

"It is, Governor," said Cornelius, shaking hands, "I've been investigating this case for quite some time. I'm hoping that our man here can fill in a few gaps."

"We've got him just down the hall," said Fraser, indicating, "Would you like some refreshment before you begin, Inspector?"

"No I'm fine thank you; I'd prefer to get on with it."

Fraser led Armstrong twenty paces along the metal platform and entered a room which the policeman suspected was used regularly for such an exercise. "I'll leave you to it Inspector," he said, holding the door open, before returning to his office.

Inside was a prison guard who sat by the door. In the middle of the room, sitting at a wooden table, was a thick-set man with dark bristles protruding from his head and chin. He was manacled at the wrists and presumably the ankles. On his forearms were blurred, faded tattoos, while his hands were grimy and his fingernails pitted. Whereas Armstrong had witnessed many villains with the customary scar on their face, this was the first time he had seen one with an open wound. It ran vertically from his forehead, across his left eye, and onto his cheek; the injury had obviously caused damage to the eye which looked bloodshot and angry. It was clear that the criminal had received the minimal amount of treatment for the apparently fresh wound that glistened in the dim light, and neither the villain himself nor the prison officials appeared surprised or overly concerned by its condition.

The policeman removed his top coat and hat and placed them on a spare chair on the other side of the room. He then slowly sat down opposite the criminal, who stared into the middle distance without acknowledging anyone. "Seamus McAllindon," said Armstrong at last.

No response. Like so many of his kind, the policeman saw that McAllindon appeared completely desensitised to what was acceptable in society.

"My name is Inspector Armstrong from the Cumberland Constabulary."

Still no response.

"I'm here looking into the death of Joseph Carter."

Again, no acknowledgement of the comment, or the name put forward.

"He's the young bloke you threw off the railway bridge at Wetheral, just outside Carlisle in June."

For the first time, McAllindon looked up at the Inspector.

"Oh, have I got your attention now?"

"I dinnea ken the man," growled McAllindon.

"Well let me remind you. Joseph Carter was a young bookies' clerk who uncovered a series of scams carried out by your old boss, Eamon Sloon."

"I dinnea ken any Sloon," interrupted McAllindon, staring hard at the policeman. Armstrong ignored the butt in.

"Sloon was an Irish racehorse trainer who was fiddling races all over the place; you were his henchman. Joseph Carter was a bright young lad who cottoned on to what Sloon was up to. He alerted the racing authorities, and Sloon was investigated and found to be behind a worldwide network of race fixing. By the time you got to Carter, it was too late to save your boss's reputation, but that didn't stop you silencing the boy."

Throughout Armstrong's reciting of the events as he saw them, McAllindon gradually lost his air of snarling contempt. His eyes gradually fixed on his accuser, and his mouth narrowly opened, apparently in search of some defence. The policeman allowed his words to sink in before his final game-clinching move.

"I believe you are currently in for grievous violence – although it seems the other bloke didn't go down without a fight," Armstrong nodded at the cut on McAllindon's face. "How long? Six months? Twelve months?"

He stood up and leaned over the table, "If I have my way son, you'll be hanging from the end of a rope before you get a chance to see the light of day again!"

"I didnea kill the boy," said the criminal at last.

"Well who did?"

"It was an accident." Armstrong said nothing and waited for McAllindon to fill the gap. "I followed him tae the wee village; it was bucketing wi' rain; he slipped on the wet bridge and knocked his brains out."

"What were you going to do, if Carter hadn't slipped?"

McAllindon dropped his head; the silence was deafening.

"There's a couple of ways we can do this, Seamus old son. Either you can say nowt and take your chances in court on a murder charge, or you can tell me everything you know about Sloon and the crooks he was dealing with – and I'll see if I can get any sentence reduced.

After another long pause, the hard man from Glasgow's east end appeared to have decided.

"Sloon worked fur some big Yank when he lost his licence he disappeared across tae America. I was told that my services were no longer needed. That's why I came back hame."

"Is the American called Neal – Solomon Neal?"

McAllindon looked blank, "I dinnae ken, I never heard Sloon mention that name."

Armstrong had long since felt the case had gone beyond the murder of a young local lad, but before he explored the other strands of his investigation, he wanted to know once and for all what had happened on that fateful June day. "So, tell me about how the young lad met his end," he said to McAllindon.

An Unwelcome Visitor

McAllindon re-appeared in Carlisle in the early months of 1911, after his employer, Sloon, had been found out in Ireland, but things had started to unravel there months before his arrival.

Completely out of the blue, in August 1910, Joseph Carter received another letter from Declan Murphy, Secretary of the Irish Jockey Club. In it, Murphy confirmed that following an initial investigation into E.L. Sloon, the Jockey Club was to launch an official investigation into the performances of his horses over the previous five seasons. It concluded by stating that '...*the Jockey Club takes a dim view of any kind of corruption in our sport and is indebted to you for bringing this matter to our attention.*'

Carter couldn't believe it. What started off as an inquisitive feeling had led to an inquiry into the background and, surely the inevitable demise, of someone who had quickly become the most successful trainer in the British Isles.

Joseph sat in his lodgings, staring blankly at the letter. It would be another month before he had cause to call to see his bookie Silas Baxter at his shop down at the Boundary. When he did call, he found Baxter in a similar distant, pre-occupied state. Unlike Carter however, he looked as though he had aged considerably since he had last seen him.

"Is everything all right, Silas?"

"Yes, I just had some worrying news, that's all," said the bookie.

"Anything I can help with?" asked Joseph, genuinely concerned for the man he had known for three years now.

"No, it's nothing we can do here," replied Baxter cryptically, staring into the middle distance.

"I have some news of my own," said the clerk in an effort to bring round his part time employer. "Can you remember last year when I was asking about that horse, Champagne Charlie?"

"What?" Baxter looked as though he'd been roused from a stupor.

"There was a horse at last year's Spring Meeting called Champagne Charlie – it was trained by that Irish bloke, Sloon."

For the first time, Silas looked at his clerk. "What about it?"

"Well I don't know if you can remember, but it flopped badly after being heavily backed. But then it won big at Newmarket later in the year."

Baxter looked at Carter with increasing incredulity. He said nothing which made Joseph feel obliged to continue.

"Then there was this other horse – Orlando. It followed a similar pattern, flopping first and then winning big." Still nothing from Baxter but an open-mouthed stare. "They were both trained by Sloon, you see. It turns out that they were only two of a number of horses from his stable who were doing the same thing. I wrote to the Irish Jock-"

"You did what!" interrupted Baxter, exploding from his dazed state.

"I..."

"You don't know what you've done!"

"What do you mean?" asked Carter, confused by the change in Baxter's mood.

The bookie's eyes shifted around the room nervously. "You'll have to go," he said suddenly.

"Silas, I don't und-"

"GO BOY! Go! Just go."

The strange meeting, and the resignation in Baxter's voice, stayed with Carter for some time, but as it was now the close season, he didn't see anything more of Silas, and he gradually let the matter pass. That was until early March 1911 when the Carlisle Journal carried the story that, following the Irish Jockey Club enquiry, E.L. Sloon had been found guilty of race fixing and banned from training.

Carter again went to visit Silas Baxter, but found his shop locked up and in darkness. Several similar attempts to make contact ended with similar findings. As the Spring Meeting 1911 approached, Joseph finally located Baxter who appeared even more agitated than the last time they had met.

"I'm not feeling too well, Joseph," he said. "I don't think I can make the meeting this year."

"What is it Silas? I've been round loads of times and your shop has always been locked up."

"Yes, I haven't been well. I think I'm going to have to pack this game in. I have some relatives who live down south; I think I might move down there."

"I'm sorry to hear that," was the best Carter could come up with.

"You get yourself away Joseph. I'll let you know how I get on." Baxter ushered the young man to the door and bid him farewell with a weak handshake. The bewildered clerk left the bookies' shop trying to make sense of Baxter's state of mind.

Unknown to him, as he was holding the conversation with Silas in the front of the shop, Seamus McAllindon was in the room behind the counter. The Scot had arrived earlier in the day demanding answers.

During the hearing into Sloon's race-fixing, it had come to light that the original suspicion into his actions had been raised through a tip-off from someone in Carlisle, Cumberland. In Sloon's mind – and therefore in McAllindon's – this could only be Silas Baxter, the bookie who had been in on the racket.

Three years earlier, Sloon had been looking for somewhere quiet and out of the way to store his ill-gotten gains from around the country. During one of his trips to Carlisle, he had found digs with Baxter, and after a quiet night's drinking with his host, one subtle hint led to another, and by the end of the night, the two had developed a clear understanding – one which would prove mutually beneficial.

As the months went by, Sloon satisfied himself that Carlisle was the perfect location: the required unassuming location with good railway links to Liverpool and Stranraer where the money could be moved over to Ireland without any suspicion before being shipped across to America. Before long, the Irishman had even arranged for funds from the continent to be held in Carlisle until the dust settled and Sloon and his American master were satisfied that the figurative and literal coast was clear in order to ship the money across the Atlantic.

"Who was that?" snarled McAllindon at the bookie after the young bemused clerk left his shop.

"Nobody," replied the beleaguered shop owner.

The villain from Glasgow's east end turned his attention back to Baxter, "As I w'sayin' what d'ye ken about Sloon being caught?"

"I don't know anything," pleaded the bookie, "why would I cause trouble for you and Eamon when I was making money myself?"

"The Jockey Club said they heard aboot the fiddles wi' a tip-off frae Carlisle."

With the menacing figure hovering over him, Silas was beside himself with fear. He held his arm above his head to protect himself from what he felt was the inevitable physical assault. The fact that it didn't come simply exacerbated Baxter's fear, as his anticipation was enough to send him into terrified convulsions.

"I lost more than that," growled McAllindon, "I lost ma job. Now that Sloon's oot the picture, he's gone tae America and told me ma services are nae longer needed."

Baxter knew when Carter had told him of his actions back in August, that there would be repercussions for them both. Would Carter have reported his findings if he knew Baxter was involved? Should Baxter have involved Carter at an earlier stage and bought his silence? Sloon was a practical man – he would have understood.

But it was all too late now. Carter had inadvertently contacted the Jockey Club, Sloon had been found out, and his vengeful henchman was now seeking recompense.

"Well if it wasnae you, who else could it h'been?" shouted McAllindon at the pathetic creature, who was now being held by the collar as he begged for mercy on his knees in the middle of his shop. Baxter's constant pleading and attempts to convince McAllindon that he was no longer holding any of Sloon's money fell on deaf ears. As he peered up at his attacker, he involuntarily glanced towards the door, through which his clerk had left some minutes earlier.

"What? Who?" snarled the Glaswegian, "...the boy?"

Baxter dropped his head in shame, knowing there was no other way but to confess, and in so doing, drag the unsuspecting Carter into the net that was closing around him.

"Who's the boy?" questioned the villain.

"He was my clerk," said Silas shamefully.

"Did he ken what was happenin'?"

Silas nodded. "He worked out the pattern concerning Eamon's horses and wrote to the Jockey Club. He didn't know that I was involved."

McAllindon dropped Baxter, who slumped to the floor. "Where dis he stay?" he asked menacingly.

Silas knew it was futile to resist. "He has digs on London Road – just opposite Cowan and Sheldon."

McAllindon was already on his way to the door, and over his shoulder he barked, "I'll be back fur what am owed after a deal wi' the boy."

The Fate of Joseph Carter

When Joseph Carter left the bookie's shop on that March morning, he struggled to understand Baxter's deteriorating physical and mental state. He slowly wandered to the junction where the five road ends met and decided to go back and press Silas for some answers. As he approached the shop, he saw the two figures inside. Baxter was on his knees as a big man stood over him with a clenched fist above his head, seemingly prepared to slam down a blow on the poor man beneath.

Carter quickly stepped back against the side of the window – enough to keep out of sight, but still close enough to see what was going on inside. He watched in prurient horror for four or five minutes until the big man let go of Baxter who slumped to the floor. Carter scampered across the road and hid in the doorway of a shop opposite, where he could see the big man leave the shop and stride off in the direction of town.

Once he was happy that the man was heading over St Nicholas' Bridge, Joseph inched his way back over the road to his, now former, employer's shop. He slipped inside and locked the door behind him. Baxter was on the floor sobbing.

"Silas, what on earth is going on?"

Baxter looked up in surprise, apparently not having heard the young man enter. "*Joseph!*" In light of the threat posed by McAllindon, Silas was amazed to see Joseph in one piece, so soon after the Glasgow villain's departure.

Carter helped Baxter to his feet and into the back room where he could make him a cup of tea and allow him to regain some composure.

Over the hot drink, Baxter told Carter everything: how he had met Sloon by chance some years earlier, and how the subsequent events had unfolded. Sloon was in the employ of an American who had a history of running such horse racing fixes; his skill appeared to be pulling the strings of people like Sloon whilst always keeping himself at a sufficient distance so as not to place himself under suspicion. "I don't even know his name," said Silas.

"I think I do," said Carter, almost to himself, recalling his hours of research.

His comment didn't register with the shocked Baxter. "The man you just saw is Seamus McAllindon. He had links to Sloon through his Irish family, but he himself is actually from Scotland – from the east end of Glasgow. He acted as Sloon's protection man, but now that Eamon has been found out and packed off to America, McAllindon is out of a job and has come looking for revenge."

At the conclusion of Baxter's narrative, Carter sat in wide-eyed astonishment. "Silas, why didn't you tell me this earlier? I tried bringing it to your attention many times and you just fobbed me off. I would never have pursued the matter if I knew it would put you in danger."

"It's not only me who's in danger lad." Baxter's expression said everything.

"*Me?*"

"I couldn't help but tell him Joseph – I had no choice!"

Carter's expression changed from astonishment to one of fear. "What should I do?" he asked, as much to himself as Baxter.

"You have to be careful Joseph – McAllindon is coming looking for you. If you can, get away for a few days."

Joseph rose to leave, "Will you be alright?"

"Yes, yes," said Baxter with a dismissive wave, "I'm beyond hope. You get yourself away and look after yourself."

Carter left the shop and cautiously followed the path trod by McAllindon less than an hour earlier. He loitered opposite his lodgings for a while before deciding it was safe to go in. As soon as he did so, he was greeted by his landlady Mrs. MacPherson who was in a terrible state of agitation. "Oh Mr. Carter, there was a big ugly Scotchman looking for you! I didn't like the look of him. He said he would be back later."

Carter knew time was short. "Mrs. MacPherson, I'm sorry for the trouble. I have to go away for a few days. If the man comes back, just tell him I won't be back for a while. And please don't tell him where I work."

The landlady agreed with an uncertain nod, and Carter hastily went up to his rooms to pack a bag.

He did leave his lodgings, but rather than leave Carlisle, he arranged for some temporary accommodation in lodgings next door to his girlfriend Jenny Little just off Botchergate. From there, he was close enough to keep an eye on his permanent address and sure enough, on no fewer than three occasions over the next two days, he saw McAllindon banging on the door, asking Mrs. MacPherson about his whereabouts. Because she genuinely believed him to be away from the city, she clearly convinced the villain that there was little point in him continuing his seemingly fruitless search.

After the third visit, Carter followed McAllindon from a discreet distance, as he finally appeared to be giving up his quest and heading towards the railway station. Once there, the young man bought a platform ticket and slunk into the shadows under the main bridge in the station and waited for the northbound London to Glasgow train to arrive. With a huge sigh of relief, he saw McAllindon climb aboard.

"What is going on Joseph," asked Jenny when he returned to his temporary lodgings.

"I'm sorry for worrying you sweetheart," replied Joseph. "I was trying to avoid a man called McAllindon, but I've just seen him get on a train for Glasgow. Everything should be alright now."

"But I don't understand, what did he want with you?"

"It's a long story but it's over with now. There's nothing to worry about."

Carter's assessment of the situation proved accurate for the following three months, but as Race Week approached in 1911– unbeknown to him and Baxter – McAllindon's financial position worsened one hundred miles north, and the villain decided to visit Carlisle once again to seek recompense for his misfortune.

It was the day of King George V's coronation, and the city was bedecked with bunting. Sadly the weather had not kept its side of the bargain; a fierce storm had battered the surrounding area the day before, and black clouds still hung threateningly overhead as McAllindon emerged from the station into Court Square.

Joseph had arranged to visit his brother and his wife at their home in the station house at Wetheral that afternoon. They had arranged to have tea together and celebrate the national day. Because of the storm, communication links had been broken, and the younger brother was unsure as to whether the arrangements had changed. But because he hadn't heard anything to the contrary, he decided to make the short train ride anyway.

McAllindon called at Carter's lodgings again to be greeted by the surprised face of Mrs. MacPherson. "Oh, it's you again!" she said remembering their encounters of a few months earlier.

The villain didn't waste time on pleasantries, "Is he in?" he barked.

"No he is not!" she said indignantly. "I'll tell him you called, now get off my step before I have the police on you!" she added, slamming the door in his face.

The Glasgow criminal then assumed the subversive role played by Carter during McAllindon's last visit to the city. He waited opposite, in the shadow of the high imposing walls of Cowan and Sheldon's crane yard, and watched for the young man to return.

A young man did return half an hour or so later. He entered the house with a key and closed the door behind him. Inside, Mrs. McPherson was in the back yard taking her sodden washing in and didn't hear the door go. Carter was late for his train, and quickly bounded up the stairs to grab a few things before dashing off for the station.

He descended the stairs as quickly as he shot up them, and just as he did so his landlady re-entered the rear of the house and saw Joseph as he was running out of the front door. "Mr. Carter! *MR. CARTER!*" she stood yelling from the front door, but it was too late to attract the attention of her lodger who was now running towards the bottom of Botchergate and out of earshot.

Across the road, Seamus McAllindon observed the whole scene and smiled as he heard the woman calling after the boy. He was satisfied that he had finally found the young man who had indirectly caused him so much trouble. It was now *his* turn to follow Carter to the station.

Keeping a distance – as Carter had done with him previously – McAllindon watched as the clerk bought a ticket and walked toward the platform from where the east-bound Newcastle train was due to depart. After he was safely out of sight, McAllindon approached the ticket booth, "Aam goin' tae the same place as that young man," he said to the man behind the counter.

"Return to Wetheral it is then sir," said the ticket official.

The Tying up of Loose Ends

"And then what happened?" Cornelius Armstrong sat in the small dark room in Barlinnie Gaol listening patiently to Seamus McAllindon's version of the events, as he knew them.

"I followed the boy to the wee village – he didnea see me as I got on the carriage behind him."

While the two were on the train, the heavens opened and another downpour ensued. The train pulled into Wetheral station and Joseph jumped off to scamper along the platform the few yards to his brother's house. Little did he know that his brother had been called away to man the nearby Cumwhinton Station while the damaged lines were being repaired. Little did he know either that Seamus McAllindon got off the train not fifty yards behind him from the rear carriage.

The big man stood on the platform, oblivious to the pouring rain that was so heavy that it actually reduced visibility. Through the torrent of water, that had all the appearance of fine platinum rods that angle down and bounced off the concrete, McAllindon waited and watched until Carter's futile door-knocking ceased.

Finally Joseph turned, annoyed that neither John nor Bridget were in, and furious that he was now helpless to shield himself from the relentless downpour. He put his head down and decided to dash for the shelter further back along the platform. Suddenly, after a few paces, he stopped with a jolt when he saw the figure along the platform through the deluge – he was just standing there facing him. Puzzled as to why someone would be just standing there in the pouring rain, when the shelter was less than ten yards from where he was standing, Carter took a few steps forward, partly to continue towards the shelter and partly to see if he could be of any assistance to the man.

When he was within ten paces, he stopped again. Suddenly, the stark realisation of who it was, and what it meant, hit him like a thunderbolt. Momentarily he was paralysed with fear, until some instinct from deep within screamed *'RUN!'*

Carter turned and ran in the opposite direction along the platform and passed his brother's house; unthinking he was running onto the metallic viaduct footpath that spanned the half mile across the Eden one hundred feet up towards Great Corby on the other side of the river.

McAllindon set off after him. Although bigger and more cumbersome, the threat of his pursuer and the realisation that his flight was futile combined to slow the young clerk down.

"He went to turn round as he w'running." McAllindon looked earnestly at Armstrong as he concluded his tale. "The metal treads were slippy wi' the rain and as he turned he went down and braed his heed on the bridge." He lowered his tone, "He were deed right away. There were a greet gash in the boy's heed."

"So what happened then?" Armstrong knew exactly when happened but he wanted to hear McAllindon say it.

"The blood was pouring out of the boy's heed as quick as the rain were fallin' frae the sky. As the rain hit the metal footpath it washed the blood away between the open treads.

"I panicked, picked the lad up and fired him the top. That way there were no sign that anything had happened there. I then decided to get back to Glasgow as quick as I could, never thinking I would be connected."

"Much to Baxter's relief, I'm sure."

McAllindon didn't respond to the reference to the Carlisle bookie, but instead explained to the Carlisle policeman how his home city became embroiled in the global swindle in the first place. "Sloon told me that it was the Yank who came to him with the ideas for fiddling various races," he concluded.

Armstrong left Glasgow that afternoon to return home. *So,* he thought to himself with a sense of irony, *it was an accident after all!* He had solved Carter's death once and for all, but Baxter, the dirty money, and this mysterious American all represented loose ends that Armstrong was intent on tying up.

It was late afternoon by the time he arrived back in Carlisle, and with no messages at the police station Cornelius went home to Abbey Street. His landlady was there in a state of excitement as he walked in.

"There's a telegram for you, Mr. Armstrong. One of the men brought it round from the police station earlier – they didn't want you to miss it." She wiped her hands on her pinny and picked up the message that she had put on the hall dresser earlier. Pausing for effect, she announced as she handed it over, "From America if you please…*New York*," with a nod and downturned mouth.

Armstrong's eyes lit up, not at the fact that this was the first correspondence he had ever received from America, but at the exciting prospect of reading its contents. "Thank you, Mrs. Wheeler," he said hurrying towards the stairs, "thank you very much indeed!"

Back in the sanctuary of his room once more, Cornelius sat at his desk studying the contents of the telegram. It was from a Wilson Hargreave of the New York Police Bureau, the contact Inspector Mather had referred to in his telephone conversation with Cornelius the previous day. His brief note would prove a seminal moment in Armstrong's investigation:

After note from Mather stop Neal unknown stop HR could be Hyman Rothstein Rochester NY stop Long suspected of race fixing in America end

Armstrong sat looking at the words on the sheet, in a state of incredulity. *HR Rochester: could it be – HR from Rochester? Hyman Rothstein from Rochester, New York? Is he the 'big Yank?' But if that's the case, then who is this Solomon Neal?*

As he was sitting there twisting the horns of his mustache in idle contemplation there was a knock at the door. "Your visitor is here," said young Emma. Armstrong heard the sound of Reuben's foot on the stairs, but before he made it to the landing his tiny black pug scampered past the young girl – making little scratching noises on the wooden floor as he did so – and into the room.

"*Athos!*" cried Cornelius, grabbing the little dog and giving him an affectionate rub on the chops. Every time the dog saw the policeman it was as if it remembered the act of kindness Cornelius once showed him. Its master followed him into the room, "Hello Reuben. Thank you Emma." The young girl shut the door and left them to it.

"I did call yesterday Mr. Armstrong," said Hanks "but you weren't in."

"Yes, Mrs. Wheeler said you called," said the policeman, remembering her description of Hanks and the effect his face would have on small children.

"I spoke to that bloke Dawson the other night. He told me that he worked for this bloke Neal who is staying with Silas Baxter. Said he'd never met him before he started working for him."

"Did he know Baxter or anything about racing?" asked Armstrong.

"No, said he just got the job by chance. Stays with his auntie in Caldewgate while his boss stays with Baxter."

"Did he know anything about Sloon?"

"No, never met the bloke."

Armstrong thought for a while. "What do you know about this McAllindon, Reuben – I saw him today in Glasgow."

Reuben looked surprised, "You have been busy Mr. Armstrong! Not much really, other than he's a real head case. You'd rather have him on your side than the other."

"Yes, that's what I thought," said Cornelius, almost to himself. "Well thank you Reuben, you've been a great help as usual." He ushered Hanks towards the door and gave Athos another affectionate rub, "The young girl will show you out."

"Night Mr. Armstrong." For his part, Reuben knew his favour to the policeman was money in the bank, as far as he was concerned, and he went home happy.

Cornelius, meanwhile, had something to eat and then sat down again with all of the information he had available: the racing periodicals, the contents of Joseph Carter's small box, and the telegram from Wilson Hargreave.

He first referred to Carter's list of horses and jockeys to see if he could decipher a pattern.

The Millionaire – CC
Eastern Seaboard – MS
Champagne Charlie – SM
Orlando – CB
In For A Penny – HC
Nickels and Dimes – PS
The Luck of the Irish – KC
Half a Sixpence – DS
d'Artagnan – PM
Amir – AC
Prince's Fare – YO
The Gambler – AS

H.R. Rochester

He already knew after speaking with Claude Irwin that In for a Penny had won the Cumberland Plate and Half a Sixpence the Derby. He decided to use these two horses as his starting point, study the various editions of the *Racing Times,* and work back from the dates of their illustrious victories. He found that in the season In For A Penny won the Plate, it flopped earlier in the Hexham Cup, after being heavily backed. Half a Sixpence meanwhile had done the same thing in the Doncaster Stakes.

Armstrong lit a pipe and reached for another paper, but then stopped and again looked at the names of the horses and the races. *In For A Penny – HC, Hexham Cup; Half a Sixpence – DS, Doncaster Stakes.* "That's it!" he said out loud, "they're not the names of the jockeys, they're the names of the races!"

And so it went on: Luck of the Irish – KC, flopped in the Kelso Cup, then won the Two Thousand Guineas; Orlando – CB, flopped in the Carlisle Bells but won the St Leger.

As the hours went by, Cornelius discovered that the fixes were far and wide: The Millionaire – CC, the Chicago Cup, and victorious in the Kentucky Derby; d'Artagnan – the Prix Morny, and then won Prix de l'Arc de Triomphe; and even Amir – AC, scratched from the Adelaide Cup before winning the more prestigious Melbourne Cup in Australia.

Armstrong sat back in the chair. *So this American – possibly Rothstein – is pulling all the strings while Sloon is training the horses and picking the races. But who the hell is this Solomon Neal?*

He reached for the piece of paper with all the names written on it. "Eamon L Sloon," he muttered to himself.

"Eamon L Sloon."

He looked at the name below. *Solomon Neal. E L Sloon...Solomon Neal... Eamon Liam Sloon...Solomon Neal.*

Then again out loud, "Eamon L Sloon...Solomon Neal." He tapped the paper with the stem of his cherry wood pipe.

"You crafty bugger!" he said with a smile of realisation.

A Painful Discovery

Believing Eamon Sloon was still in Carlisle, and staying with Silas Baxter, Inspector Armstrong wasted no time the following morning making his way to the bookie's shop down Boundary.

Frustratingly, like his previous visits, he found the establishment locked up and in total darkness. He cupped his hands to the side of his face and pressed up against the window to see if he could make out anything on the inside – nothing. Futile rapping on the door was followed by a wander round into the back lane in the vain attempt to gain access, or at least to see any signs of life.

Surely if Michael Dawson was still in Carlisle, then the man he was employed to protect would be too, thought Armstrong. It just didn't make sense – *unless Sloon and Baxter had used Dawson's presence as a decoy, and fled the city.*

Cornelius went back around the front and decided to ask at the news agent's shop next door if they had seen anyone.

"I saw Silas only yesterday," said the man behind the counter, "it's the first I've seen of him for a long time."

"How did he seem?" asked the policeman.

"A bit distant – said something about his bank account, but he was rambling to be honest. I couldn't make head nor tail of him."

"Has anyone been staying with him, do you know?"

"Now you mention it, I have seen a bloke with a black beard once or twice. I just assumed he was a relative. As I say, I haven't had much craik with him lately."

Cornelius thanked the newsvendor. Once outside, he took one last look at the unlit shop next door, and decided to go back into town. He decided on impulse to visit the National Bank on the corner of English

Street and Bank Street. As it was the biggest bank in the city, Armstrong speculated that this is where a businessman like Silas Baxter might hold his considerable amount of money.

After being shown to the manager George Moulding's office, the Inspector explained the reason for his visit, and asked if Baxter held an account at the branch. Moulding seemed a little nonplussed.

"He *did*, Inspector. My senior clerk showed him into my office only yesterday and explained that Mr. Baxter intended to close both of the accounts he held with us."

"Did he explain why?" asked Armstrong.

"He didn't go into detail as to why; he mentioned something about going away. I explained to him that we could always transfer his funds to another branch elsewhere in the country, but he was adamant that he wanted to withdraw all of the contents and close the accounts immediately." It was clear that the Bank Manager wasn't terribly impressed by losing such custom.

"Can I ask how much Mr. Baxter held in his accounts?" The policeman's question added to Moulding's discomfort and he twisted in his seat. "It is very important Mr. Moulding," added Armstrong, "part of my official enquiries."

"In excess of ten thousand pounds," said Moulding after a long pause.

If Armstrong was in any doubt beforehand about how involved Baxter was in the huge swindle, he was in no doubt now. A small bookie from Carlisle could never hope to handle that sort of money, and part of him wanted to know why Moulding wouldn't question such sums being deposited. There was no time for that however; Cornelius thanked the banker and left.

Before returning to the police station, he visited Tullie House where the Head Librarian Sydney Irvine had indirectly helped him with his enquiries on many occasions. On this occasion, the Inspector wanted to consult the archive copies of *The Times*, to see if he could find out any information about the mysterious Hyman Rothstein. The New York policeman said that Rothstein had been suspected of wrongdoing for some time – might there be a chance that something had made the newspapers over the past few years?

Irvine showed Armstrong to his usual researching area and sat him down with a pile of selected newspapers with various dates covering the previous five years. "That should keep you quiet for an hour or two, Inspector," he said.

"Thank you Sydney," replied the policeman with a smile.

As daunting a task as it appeared to be, Cornelius knew exactly what he was looking for: he was gambling by scouring the 'World News' sections of the various newspapers, something might be recorded about Rothstein or his activities.

After forty minutes, Armstrong's patience was rewarded with a piece in the 20 March, 1909 edition that referred to:

New York businessman Hyman Rothstein was released without charge today by a Federal Board of Investigation that is investigating suspected financial wrongdoing in the sports of Baseball, Boxing and Horse Racing. Mr. Rothstein, who lives in Rochester, New York, said he would not be pursuing claims of compensation for his wrongful detention. Investigations continue into what has been described as the biggest sporting-related swindle ever known in the United States. Six men remain in custody regarding the matter.

Back at the police station, Inspector Armstrong completed his log book for Monday 8 April 1912, including his visit to Barlinnie Gaol to see Seamus McAllindon, and started today's entry by recording his interview with the Bank Manager. He then briefed his Chief Constable Henry Baker on the latest situation.

"I have proof now, Henry, that young Joseph Carter uncovered, by chance, the activities of the Irish trainer Eamon Sloon and the bookie Silas Baxter, who was holding the dirty money at his shop. When it was quiet, Sloon would arrange for the money to be shipped over to America to the mastermind of the whole thing – this Rothstein character. When Carter contacted the Irish Jockey Club, they investigated further and banned Sloon, who dispensed with the services of McAllindon before going to America.

"McAllindon then comes back to Carlisle and poor Carter's fate is sealed as a result. Sloon, meanwhile, goes to America, where he stays for a few months before re-surfacing in the guise of the little known American trainer Solomon Neal: a bit of padding, blackened hair and a beard, along with a new henchman who has never met Sloon before, and the whole fixing process starts again. The frustrating thing is that I think we've just missed Sloon and Baxter as they seem to have fled Carlisle only yesterday – with an awful lot of money."

Baker rubbed his chin after his Inspector's narrative. "This is excellent work Cornelius. If only we knew the whereabouts of the bookie and his partner in crime, we could tie the case up completely."

Armstrong left his superior's office and spent the afternoon pondering how he could apprehend Sloon and Baxter and recover the money that the latter had cleared from his bank account the previous day. Going over the lengthy case in his mind until he was virtually the last one left in the station, his deliberations were broken when a young telegram boy came into the station with another cable from New York. The Inspector ripped open the telegram to find another note from Wilson Hargreave, who had obviously done some further investigation following the enquiries from his English colleagues:

Rothstein sailed to England to travel back on the new White Star liner End

The White Star liner? Armstrong then remembered his meeting with James Bell's cousin some days ago. He rose from his desk and reached into his overcoat pocket which hung on the stand by the door. He pulled out the leaflet that Bell had given to him and glanced through it again. When he came to the list of VIPs he stared in incredulity:

Colonel John Astor, New York City, NY – Property Developer
Mr. Mauriz Hakan Bjornstrom-Steffansson, Stockholm, Sweden – Businessman
Mr Paul Romaine Marie Léonce Chevré, Paris, France - Sculptor

Dr Washington Dodge, San Francisco, California – Politician
Colonel Archibald Gracie IV, Washington DC – Writer
Mr Hyman Rothstein, Rochester, NY – Businessman
Mr Joseph Bruce Ismay, Liverpool, England – Ship owner
Mr Colonel (Oberst) Alfons Simonius-Blumer, Basel, Switzerland – Banker'

ROTHSTEIN! He's here! Armstrong suddenly realised that this is why Sloon had stayed with Baxter for so long. If they were in the employ of Rothstein, could it be that they were going to join their mastermind and travel with him in some style to the safety of the United States?

Armstrong's satisfaction at tying up the final loose ends of the case was tempered by the fact that it was probably too late to make enquiries with his colleagues in the south, or on the railway, in order to raise the alarm concerning Sloon and Baxter; and without their apprehension, there was no chance of snaring the master criminal Rothstein.

After a little thought, and after sending desk sergeant Bill Townsend home, he decided to clutch at a last straw and make another visit to Baxter's shop in the vain hope that the bookie and the trainer might still be there.

Catching a tram to the bottom of Botchergate, Armstrong walked over St Nicolas Bridge as dusk approached. Unknown to him, about quarter of a mile over the bridge, Baxter and Sloon – still in the guise of Solomon Neal – were preparing their flight.

After lying low for several days they were ready to leave Carlisle for the last time. While the two packed the money into bags in the back room of the bookie's shop, Sloon decided the time was right for a little celebration. "How about we treat ourselves to a couple of bottles of beer, Silas? Your last in this sad little place!" Baxter hadn't the energy or the inclination to agree nor disagree – he simply shrugged his ambivalence to his friend, who volunteered, "I'll go and get some bottles from the 'Currock,' while you pack the rest of the money."

Sloon left the shop quietly, swinging the door shut behind him without looking, and headed for the *Currock Inn*, only a few hundred yards up one of the adjoining roads. He didn't realise however, as he walked away, that the door didn't have the momentum to close properly; instead the latch lightly bumped gently against the keeper and rested slightly ajar.

Coincidentally, as Sloon disappeared from view, Cornelius Armstrong walked towards Silas Baxter's shop expecting his journey to be fruitless. He repeated his action of earlier that day by cupping his hands around his eyes to peer through the window into the blackness; and like earlier that day, he saw nothing.

Almost as an afterthought, he motioned to knock on the door, and was amazed to see that it was standing ajar. Not believing his luck he eased the door gently open and stepped inside. All was quiet and strangely eerie. Armstrong paced silently towards the rear of the shop and through the raised hatch and behind the counter. His heart skipped a beat as he heard a noise coming from the room beyond. Easing his way towards the doorway, he looked round the door jamb. Inside was Silas Baxter on his knees packing bundles of notes into Gladstone bags that stood on the floor. On the table above him were more bundles of notes – Armstrong noticed they were not only pounds sterling but French francs, Italian lira and even Australian dollars.

The policeman finally gave up his hiding place and stepped into the doorway and into view, "Silas Baxter I presume?"

The bookie looked up in horror, his weasel features suggesting that his nerves were completely shredded.

Armstrong stepped into the room and stood looking from the bookie to the money and back again. "So where is your friend Neal – or should I say Sloon?"

A split-second before it all went black he heard a soft Irish voice that came from behind: "He's here!"

An Unpredictable Twenty-Four Hours Ahead

The moments immediately prior to awakening are often beautiful and gentle, as the instant recollection of a good night's sleep is complemented by the thought of a lovely morning or an exciting day ahead. On this occasion however, the moment was full of blurry blacks and purples and greens. And pain.

The prone Cornelius Armstrong came to and the room gradually focused around him. The moment he tried to lift his face off the gritty floor and ease himself upright, a searing pain forced him to a state of collapse and almost pushed him back into unconsciousness. He instinctively reached for the back of his head and groaned with the pain.

Lying there in the dimly lit room, Cornelius remembered his encounter with Baxter before blacking out – he now realised why he had blacked out as his senses gradually cleared. He opened his eyes and, by gently moving one limb at a time, managed to lever himself up on to one of the wooden chairs that stood in the middle of the room. He groaned again at the effort and slumped over the matching table to recover.

Unsure as to how long he had been unconscious, Armstrong continued to recall the events prior to this. the revelation about Sloon and Neal; the correspondence with the Irish Jockey Club; the telegrams from New York; and his finding Baxter red-handed with bags full of different currencies.

As soon as Cornelius could raise the alarm, the two fugitives would soon to be wanted all over the British Isles; the policeman now believed more than ever that the two were planning to meet with Hyman Rothstein in order to make a dash for it across the Atlantic to the sanctuary of the American's homeland.

As his mind cleared, he remembered Doctor Bell's cousin telling him about the White Star liner that would be leaving on 10th April. The activity inside Armstrong's skull suddenly gave way to discomfort on the surface – he winced again at the shooting pain. He realised he could do with seeing Doctor Bell for two reasons.

Unaware of the time of day, but assuming it was the morning of the 10th, he leant on the table and gingerly got up from his chair. Once upright, he waited for the room to settle down before trying to find a way out of Baxter's shop. Unsurprisingly, the villains had locked all the doors behind them so that Cornelius had to first re-orientate himself with the ground floor of the premises and then find a way out of the damn place.

The heavy door that divided this back room and the front shop was not going to be barged open – especially in his delicate state. Instead, he turned his attention to an adjoining door that crashed open with a couple of hard kicks with the sole of his boot. After a moment of hanging onto the door frame to compose himself, he entered what was a small kitchen which, he was pleased to find, had a window into the back yard.

Climbing onto the Belfast sink, Armstrong pulled his coat above his face and put his elbow to the window. The glass shattered easily, and with a little more clearing of the shards around the frame, Cornelius created enough of an aperture to escape the building. By clambering onto the coal bunker, he managed to shinny over the back wall into the lane that serviced the whole of the terraced properties.

Checking his watch for the first time, he saw it was after eleven o'clock. The criminals had over fourteen hours start on him, but first Cornelius knew he had to see Doctor Bell.

Amid the bustling little shopping area of the Boundary, a disheveled Police Inspector climbed onto an omnibus heading back into the city centre. His fellow passengers were either oblivious or disinterested in his condition. "This is the Boundary!" yelled the conductor, much to Armstrong's discomfort, "next stop, St Nic!"

The policeman actually alighted at the railway station further on; his purpose was to establish if two men had caught the sleeper to London the previous night. Waving away the stationmaster's concerns about his appearance, Armstrong discovered that they had bought a one-way ticket, with a connection in the capital to Southampton. Cornelius wasted no time in jumping in a hansom for the second half of his journey up to the Cumberland Infirmary.

Fortunately, he found James Bell washing up, preparing to eat his mid-day sandwiches. Cornelius often wondered how the Doctor could eat surrounded by cadavers and the stench from the morgue, but now wasn't the time to go into that.

"What happened to you?" cried Bell as the Inspector came in.

"I was knocked out last night," replied Armstrong, and then, before the Doctor could enquire further, "James, I need your help with two issues. First, can you do anything with this?" he leaned forward and bowed his head to give the medical man a better look at the wound. Bell grimaced and sucked in air through his pierced lips at the sight of the laceration and the dried blood that caked Armstrong's hair to his skull. "I'm sure you've seen worse," said Cornelius.

"Yes, but I don't usually engage in conversation with my normal clients," replied Bell. "I'm a pathologist, not a general medic."

"Surely you can clean it up and dress it for me?"

"Certainly," said Bell, "bear with me and I'll go and get some swabs."

While he was gone, Cornelius sat in silence wondering how he could prevent Baxter and Sloon getting away with thousands of pounds of ill-gotten gains.

Bell returned momentarily and started dressing the policeman's wound. "You said there were two issues?" he asked.

"Yes. I remember the conversation we were having with your cousin when I came to see you a couple of weeks ago. He is the Chief Engineer on that trans-Atlantic vessel."

Bell looked up at the large clock in the morgue – it was five minutes to mid-day. "It's funny you should mention it. As we speak this minute, Joseph and his crew will be stoking her up – she'll be weighing anchor in five minutes. Terribly excited he was," mused Bell. "Why do you ask?"

"I believe the men that did this to me are on that ship heading for America. Whatsmore, they have thousands of pounds and other currencies with them, fiddled through horse-racing scams around the world."

Bell looked aghast before offering, "I could try and get a message to Joseph through the White Star office – the ship has some extremely sophisticated wireless and telephone equipment. Perhaps Joseph could alert the Captain and have these men apprehended. He told me the ship makes a short journey to Cherbourg before picking up the last of the passengers and cargo in Queenstown, Ireland, tomorrow."

"It would probably be easier coming from you James," said Armstrong, eagerly, "given your relations with Joseph."

Doctor Bell had virtually finished dressing the policeman's wound. "I'll contact them immediately and see if I can get hold of Joseph."

Cornelius left the Infirmary with a throbbing head but with a strange sense of optimism about the case; he had solved the demise of poor Joseph Carter and identified wrongdoing on an unimaginable scale, but how could he prevent the perpetrators of both crimes getting away and disappearing into America? He was still pondering the position as he entered the police station.

"What happened to you sir?" asked Sergeant Bill Townsend on the front desk as he saw the dressing on his superior's head.

"Never mind that," dismissed Armstrong, "have there been any messages for me?"

"None sir," said the sergeant.

The Inspector headed for the Chief Constable's office. Knocking and entering, he wasted no time in apprising his superior of the events that had occurred since the two spoke last, the previous afternoon.

"It might work out, Cornelius." Henry Baker tried to re-assure his detective. "If we wire ahead to this chap Wilson Hargeave and give him details of Sloon, Baxter and the money, he will be able to snare the whole lot of them as soon as the ship docks in New York. I suggest you do that now Inspector."

"Yes, sir," said Armstrong, not entirely convinced.

Having sent the telegram, it was half past four when Cornelius Armstrong was sitting at his desk pondering the situation. Suddenly, Doctor Bell, who he had left earlier in the afternoon, burst into his office. "Cornelius! I have news from Joseph, who has spoken personally to Captain

Smith. The Captain has contacted the port in Dublin and arranged for you to join the ship if you can make it. It means you can apprehend the villains yourself and hand them over upon arrival in America!"

Armstrong's mind was in a whirl: *how can I get to Dublin? Apprehend Sloon and Rothstein as well as Baxter! What will I need? New York! America!*

Henry Baker had left his office at the sound of the commotion and heard what Bell had said. "What are you waiting for, Cornelius?" he demanded. "Get after them! You can get the train to Liverpool tonight, the early morning ferry to Belfast, and then the train tomorrow morning to Dublin."

Armstrong found the proposal irresistible – he shook hands with the Doctor and the Chief Constable and hurried home before embarking on the trip of a lifetime that would see him make arrests that would surely be the highlight of his career.

The Fate of Cornelius Armstrong

Cornelius stood on the dockside in Liverpool waiting for the early morning ferry to Belfast. His eyes stung with tiredness from an uncomfortable night on the train south from Carlisle. The smell of the sea air and squawking of the seagulls was unnatural to the policeman and did little to alleviate to his sense of detachment.

Despite feeling subdued, Armstrong couldn't help but smile to himself as he listened to the banter from his fellow passengers – their throaty, lazy dialect reminded him of the sharp-witted lamp lighter Bobby Lloyd back home.

He looked over at the grand White Star offices on the far side of the docks. It seemed like reminders of the magnificent vessel were everywhere; during the crossing he overheard two passengers chattering about it, and no sooner did the eastern coast of Ireland come into sight than the enormous cranes in the Harland and Wolfe shipyard stood to attention, as if boasting of their achievements over the previous three years.

It transpired that many passengers from the ferry had the same intentions as Armstrong, and as he reached the foot of the gangway following the ferry's docking he overheard a quayside official giving directions towards the railway station and "…the boat train," to a group in front of him. Cornelius surmised the group was on the same mission as himself. Following the man's directions, it quickly became apparent that the dozen or so English sightseers were being joined by hundreds of their Irish counterparts.

Once on board the ten o'clock westbound train, Armstrong learned that the locals who were making the journey were the men who had built the White Star sister ships over the previous three years. They had been given permission to take the day off to travel to Dublin with their families to see the ship they had built – the biggest the world had ever seen – slip its moorings and set off on her maiden Atlantic adventure.

The atmosphere on the train was one of excitement as it rattled through the Irish countryside; that was until it reached Dundalk Station where it halted. There was nothing unusual in that of course, but when the normal three minutes turned into five, and then into seven, Cornelius sensed a changing mood amongst the passengers.

The jovial banter gradually turned into curious chatter; and when nervous whispering turned into complete silence, Armstrong knew something was terribly wrong.

With the purpose of his journey momentarily forgotten, Cornelius was alarmed to see armed men appear on the platform outside. They were dressed in civilian clothes and it seemed that they all had their flat caps pulled down over their eyes. They all carried rifles.

The passengers on board the train didn't seem to share the Englishman's surprise; instead they simply sat in silence with their heads pointed downwards.

After ten minutes of confused, incoherent shouting from the men up and down the platform, Cornelius looked out to see some of the armed men start to board the train. Within moments two men swung the door from the lobby open and walked slowly down the carriage. The tension was palpable, and the English policeman debated whether to challenge the men or not. A man sitting diagonally opposite Cornelius appeared to read his intentions and caught his eye. With wide-eyes and an almost imperceptible shake of the head, he discouraged Armstrong from his course of action. The two armed men continued to slowly pace through, peering at the passengers who sat in silent submission, before leaving the carriage at the other end to presumably repeat the same exercise.

The tension was broken somewhat when Cornelius heard a voice from a couple of seats behind mumble to a companion, "We're going to miss the damn thing at this rate."

Armstrong suddenly remembered the need for a speedy journey and pulled out his watch: it was approaching quarter to eleven.

The agony continued for another half hour, until the men apparently decided whatever they were looking for was not on the train. As the last of their number clambered down and back onto the platform, signals were relayed along to the driver to pull off. After over fifty minutes of breathing heavily in its unnatural stationary position, the locomotive chugged into action and continued its journey south west.

Once they were back underway, the man who had tacitly warned Armstrong against taking any action leaned across the aisle – it transpired that he was a regular visitor from the mainland who had become accustomed to the increasing sectarian tensions on the island. "They were nationalist – the Irish Volunteers," he explained. "They are determined to force through the Home Rule bill. They would be looking for Ulster Volunteers – the unionists.There's been talk of the Ulstermen importing arms from Germany to further their cause. It all makes for a tense atmosphere over here these days."

Armstrong recalled reading how Prime Minister Herbert Asquith had sent Winston Churchill to Belfast a few weeks earlier to appeal for calm and moderation, and nationalists had responded by attacking the First Lord of the Admiralty's car.

The two train passengers chatted about the political divide and their own respective backgrounds before the increased discomfort amongst the other passengers engulfed the carriage. With the clock ticking past one o'clock in the afternoon, they were starting to concern themselves with the fact that they might not see the ship leave. Cornelius had greater concerns: he was due to be on board the vessel as it did so.

Ten miles south west meanwhile, no such concerns existed. It was a fine, clear spring morning and the harbour at Queenstown was filled with tugs and small boats. Towering above them all stood the biggest vessel ever built. The smell of burning coal filled the air on a quayside that was a hive of activity; men loaded cargo and supplies, while thousands of awestruck onlookers waved and cheered at the lucky people on board.

With embarkation almost complete, the sound of Irish pipes came from the aft of the ship, as if to signal its imminent departure.

Titanic was an incredible sight; beyond its size, its grace and stature epitomised everything about twentieth century engineering. The four huge funnels towered against the blue sky, while its superstructure shone in the early afternoon sun. The thin gold line at the hull's upper edge proudly identified the new vessel as part of the White Star Line.

Vehicles started to be cleared from the First Class gangways as the spectators on the landing stage became frenzied in anticipation. The lucky steerage passengers who, less than an hour earlier had been amid the noise and bustle of the eating houses, shouted across to their unlucky colleagues who were missing out on the life-changing trip to the New World.

It was twenty past one when the boat train finally pulled into the station immediately adjacent to the harbour. The train disgorged its leaping passengers almost before it had stopped moving; Cornelius Armstrong ran along the platform, skipping and weaving past the slow moving hoards. Running out of the station entrance and down the sloping walkway towards the quayside, he was halted at the awesome sight of the giant vessel that was more than two hundred yards from where he was, but was so enormous it was as though he could reach out and touch it.

Before he could come to his senses and resume his sprint, his heart sank as he saw the gangways being withdrawn and the heavy mooring lines splashing into the water. Even if he could get through the roaring hundreds below, it was too late to explain his eleventh-hour invitation to the officials on the quayside, let alone board the vessel. His mind raced: *so close but so far. The embarrassment, the missed opportunity. What will happen to the villains and the money? Could he contact the New York policeman? How will he get home?*

Two tugs had come alongside to help nudge the big ship out into the stream. From the walkway Cornelius looked on helplessly at the mosaic of faces on board the ship as smoke started to plume from the liner's tall funnels. The towering black wall of iron began to move – her anchor was already aweigh, and as Armstrong watched, *Titanic's* long profile gradually shortened as her bows swung southward towards the sea. He watched as the word 'Liverpool' on the stern gradually faded, and the giant vessel eventually became a tiny speck in the distance.

As most of the onlookers turned to leave, Armstrong completed his descent from the walkway and entered the eating house on the quayside in a mixed state of shock and disappointment. The pungent odours of fried fat, vinegar and tobacco smoke did little to mitigate his frustration. The clientele inside seemed to share the Inspector's demeanor; most had a slightly shabby appearance, and it became apparent that many of them were Scandinavian and Dutch: would-be refugees dreaming of a new life in America. The fact that they were here and not on board suggested that their dream would remain unfulfilled for some time.

The man behind the counter told Cornelius that the next ferry to the mainland was at six o'clock that evening – it arrived in Anglesey at midnight. The alternative was to wait until the morning and travel back to Liverpool. Unsure of how or when he could get back to Carlisle from Wales, Cornelius decided on the second option, and took the man's offer of a room at his wife's boarding house, nearby.

The End Game

The wind howled across the surface of the Irish Sea. The ferry surged forward, bursting through the waves and creating great showers of spray that were blown over her bow. Cornelius Armstrong stood on deck, largely oblivious to the wild weather; his overcoat was covered with an oilskin to protect him from the icy squalls. What a difference from yesterday.

He had read in the morning edition of *The Irish Times* about the launch of *Titanic* and the pride of Ireland's connection with the vessel. He had also discovered the reason for his late arrival that led to him missing his adventure of a lifetime, as the newspaper reported that the morning boat train had been halted by a group of the nationalists affiliated to the Irish Republican Brotherhood who suspected the leader of the Ulster Volunteers, Edward Carson, was on the train. The paper speculated as to what their intention was if they had found Carson, but as he was not on board, the report concluded that the train was allowed to complete its journey, albeit an hour behind schedule.

Don't I know it, thought Cornelius. Rather than powering across the Atlantic in style to New York, where he would complete the most complex and prestigious case of his career, he found himself chugging back across the Irish Sea to England, where he was vulnerable to derision and further humiliation if the case could not be tied up in his absence, five thousand miles west.

It was eight o'clock on the evening of 12th April when he arrived back at his lodgings in Carlisle. Having contacted Henry Baker before leaving Dublin the previous day, the message had been relayed to Mrs. Wheeler who had a hot meal waiting for him upon his arrival.

The following morning, he was back at his desk, well aware that the most important case of his career was hanging by a thread – it had taken ten months to get to this point, and it was in danger of unraveling at the last.

"It could only happen to you, Cornelius!" Chief Constable Henry Baker couldn't help teasing his Inspector, whilst knowing his man was well capable of recovering the situation. "You need to contact the chap in New York and make sure he is ready to apprehend the crooks when they arrive."

"I know what's required, sir," said Armstrong turning to leave.

He sent a lengthy telegram to Wilson Hargreave, explaining his own misfortune but updating him on the three men he needed to arrest upon the ship's docking. He also advised the American detective that the evidence would be obtained from Baxter and Sloon in the form of the Gladstone bags full of the various currencies.

Not content with contacting Hargreave, Armstrong remembered James Bell telling him about the *Titanic's* sophisticated communications systems, and through some enquiries with the White Star office in Liverpool, he had sent a cable to the ship itself to ensure that the senior crew were fully aware of the situation and the potential dangers involved in hosting such dangerous villains and their plunder.

Late in the afternoon of Saturday 13th April 1912, Inspector Armstrong received two replies to his messages. One from Wilson Hargreave acknowledging the Carlisle man's instructions and re-assuring him that everything was in place; and a second from *Titanic* itself:

Message received Inspector stop Captain Smith fully aware and has contacted New York stop Nothing to worry about End

Jack Phillips
Senior Wireless Operator

Happy that he had done all he could, the following day Cornelius decided to visit John Carter, the stationmaster at Wetheral, to return the box belonging to his brother and to update him on his varied investigation, since he had spoken to him last, less than a month earlier.

He explained how the contents of the box – and Joseph's initial detective work – contributed to uncovering the race horse swindles that had taken place all over the world. "More than just the Carlisle Bells and Cumberland Plate fix, I'm afraid," concluded the policeman.

John and his wife Bridget were naturally upset by the Inspector's discoveries but strangely found some comfort in knowing the full story. Cornelius assured them that he would ensure that Joseph's name and reputation would be completely undamaged by the scandal that was about to be uncovered as soon as the villains arrived in America.

Before the policeman returned to Carlisle, he decided to pay young Edward Stoneycroft and his mother a visit.

"Had it not been for Edward telling me about the man falling from the bridge," he said to Amelia at the conclusion of his tale, "I would never have uncovered the truth."

"Thank you Inspector," said Mrs. Stoneycroft – and then turning to her son, "What do you think of that Edward?"

"The man fall off the bridge, I saw him from the window," was all the youngster could offer.

"He did Edward," said Cornelius offering to shake hands, "thank you very much. And thank *you* again, Mrs. Stoneycroft."

Mother and son watched from the same window and waved at the Inspector as he walked down the garden path.

All that remained now was for Inspector Armstrong to wait patiently for the next seventy-two hours until *Titanic* docked in New York and Wilson Hargreave confirmed the successful conclusion to the case.

The time passed without a word, and by Thursday 18th April, as Armstrong still hadn't heard anything, his instinct told him that something was very wrong. He decided to send a telegram to Hargreave:

Is there any news of *Titanic*

CA

At five o'clock that afternoon, a telegram boy came into the station and handed a reply to the Inspector, who ripped it open impatiently. The cryptic message read:

Too early to say stop Still searching stop *Carpathia* due to arrive later today stop Will contact again when more news available End

W Hargreave

Cornelius left that night puzzled by Hargreave's message. He even wondered if the New York policeman had mistakenly sent the telegram to him by mistake – intending it for someone else entirely. He went to bed that night feeling very uneasy about the whole confused affair.

The following morning, he was woken early by his distraught landlady who was banging on his door, "Mr Armstrong, sir, Mr Armstrong! Have you heard the terrible news?"

Cornelius levered himself into his dressing gown and opened the door, "What is it Mrs. Wheeler? What's wrong?"

She handed the newspaper to him, "Oh, all those people! All those poor people!" She left him and headed back downstairs, wringing her hands and close to tears.

Cornelius looked down at the headline of the newspaper in jaw-dropping disbelief. '*Titanic* sunk!' screamed the *Carlisle Journal* 'over a thousand lives lost.' The piece went on to relay the early reports of the tragedy, and how the *RMS Carpathia* had picked up over seven hundred survivors. Armstrong wandered back into his sitting room and slumped into his rocking chair. After several minutes, his state of shock was compounded when young Emma knocked on his door with yet another telegram from New York.

Rothstein, Baxter and Sloon not among the survivors End

W Hargreave

He thought of '…those poor people' as Mrs. Wheeler had called them; even the two criminals and the master villain – no one deserved this. And his own fate! "There but for the grace of God…" he mumbled to himself.

Once he had recovered some composure, he realised his first duty was to visit his friend James Bell.

The Kaiser's Assassin

It's War!

Doctor Alex Strickland sat at the desk of his Angel Lane surgery in Penrith staring into the middle distance. He had been aware of the approaching date for some time leading up to it, but it was only this morning when he sat down and ripped off the top sheet on his desk calendar to reveal the large red number above the smaller black letters that indicated the month that caused him to pause. The revealing of the new date was usually one of the little rituals with which he started each morning as a matter of course, to satisfy himself that he was in the right frame of mind for the day's business. This day however, as it did every year, prompted him to glaze over as his memory banks flooded with the significance of the anniversary and the subsequent events. The calendar indicated it was 11th October.

Fourteen years earlier, he had been a young games master at Queen Elizabeth's Grammar School with ambitions to combine his two passions for sport and medicine and become a pioneer in the embryonic field of studying sports-related injury.

Six weeks into the new term and Strickland had organised a rugby match between his boys and those from Nelson Thomlinson School near Wigton. The game passed without major incident, and Alex was delighted that his lads' early season training had paid off with an 18-7 victory. As the boys were leaving the muddy field and Alex was standing beside Mr Black, the proud Headmaster, the skipper of Queen Elizabeth's, gave out the traditional courteous cry after every game in honour of their opponents: "Three cheers for Nelson Thom: hip, hip-..."

During the cheering, Alex saw the figure of Science Master Mr Fitzsimmons out of the corner of his eye as he came bounding down the grassed terrace; his grey wispy hair straggling in the wind, while his black gown billowed behind him as he raced across the field waving a piece of paper above his head. Alex could see that he was shouting something, but was unable to make it out above the din of the boys until Fitzsimmons got to within twenty yards.

"Headmaster! Headmaster! It's war!"

Fitzsimmons's concern and excitement appeared lost on most of the spectators – parents, fellow pupils and a few off-duty members of staff – as they slowly dispersed from the field, idly holding a dozen or more desultory conversations.

Strickland however, listened intently to the Science Master's briefing of Mr Black. He had followed the story in the newspaper for most of the summer, sickened by the jingoistic propaganda, and as he had suspected for some time, the unnecessary war had now indeed been created with the Boers of South Africa. Minutes later, he sat on the wooden benches in the home changing room. The boys were too distracted and pleased with their victory to take much notice of their Games Master as he contemplated what the next few weeks held for him and the country.

As it was, the next two months raced by: Strickland was a member of the Volunteers and, as forces quickly became depleted on the Cape, rumours grew that part timers were to be called up to serve abroad. By Christmas, amid a patriotic fervour never before seen, one hundred thousand volunteers had been called up to swell the numbers of army personnel in South Africa. Significantly, Strickland – the best pistol shot in the group – was one of eighteen drawn from the Penrith Volunteers.

As he sat in his surgery looking at the picture of him and his colleagues leaving Penrith on their fateful mission, Strickland now thought how false hopes and foolhardiness are somehow overlooked in the jingoism of troops leaving to serve in some foreign land. He closed his eyes and remembered the send-off that the townsfolk gave him and his colleagues: the cheering crowd, the banner-strewn pathway to the station, the brass band playing *Soldiers of the Queen*.

The reality of course was very different: the oppressive conditions of the high veldt, the endless marches, and then the fighting, with all its carnage. After Boschfontein, and the inglorious return home on the hospital ship, the cruelest six months of Strickland's life were completed when he discovered that his beloved Adelaide and their unborn child had died after complications had developed during the pregnancy. Alex had left not knowing that Addy *was* pregnant; upon his return, the loss of his love and the guilt of knowing that his beautiful girl had attempted to shoulder the shame of their unmarried consummation alone, was unbearable.

Like all parents, Alex's had always encouraged him to be the best he could be: a teacher, a solicitor, or follow his father into the medical profession. Young Strickland's own dream would see him develop into sports-related medicine, leave Penrith for London, marry Addy, and become a leading authority on the new alternative area of the medical profession. But with his leg shattered, then amputated, and his love lost, he only succeeded in becoming the subject of small-town tittle-tattlers and cruel rumour-mongers.

With his career and ambitions seemingly in tatters, three years after the war, he completed his medical studies, and when his father retired two years after that he took over his surgery in the centre of Penrith, where he also lived and provided accommodation for his maid – the sister of an old friend – and his widowed housekeeper, Mrs. Brownlee.

His glazed eyes looked at the calendar again: the eleventh of October. Could he ever have imaged the significance of that date in 1899? It seemed now as though that day had been the high point of his life – everything since appeared to be a descent from that distant acme. Fourteen years – it seemed like a thousand.

The knock on the door seemed to come like a Boer shell that made him jump. His reverie had been so intense that he had temporarily forgotten where he was. He shook himself, and went to stand up in order to clear his head. Instantly, he grimaced and hissed in pain as his prosthetic leg threatened to buckle under him. He reached down and rubbed just above where the stump met the calliper then, checking his pocket watch, he took a deep breath to collect himself and straightened his jacket, hoping that his first patient would not suspect him of having just been slumped over his desk. Having resumed his dignity and his bearings, he straightened in his chair and faced the door.

"Come in."

"The Earl's here, sir," said the maid.

Not only had Strickland forgotten about his patients and the day ahead, he had overlooked the fact that his first patient was Hugh Lowther, the 5th Earl of Lonsdale. Lord Lonsdale had sustained a shoulder injury from a fall whilst hunting earlier that summer, and his own physician, Gideon Rogers – knowing Strickland's father and the younger man's interest and ability in treating sports-related injuries – recommended the Earl visit his town-centre colleague. Strickland had treated the Earl with some physiotherapy on four occasions during the summer, and this was to be his final visit.

"Thank you Violet, show him in."

"Are you sure you're all right sir," asked Violet, concerned that she had waited a long time for her employer to respond to her knock.

"Yes, I'm fine, thank you. You can show the Earl in now."

The maid bobbed a curtsey in assent.

Lord Lonsdale was a charismatic figure who had a presence and a fire in his eye that belied his fifty-five years. He not only hunted, but had been known in the past to vigorously pursue his other sporting passions: boxing and horseracing.

"Now then young Strickland," he said as he entered the surgery.

"Good morning, My Lord, and how is the shoulder?" Strickland had given Lonsdale a series of exercises to perform between visits.

"Splendid," replied the Earl, enthusiastically, "feels as right as rain."

"Let's have a look shall we," said the Doctor, encouraging his patient to remove his coat and shirt. Strickland raised the Earl's arm and manipulated the damaged area. "Any pain there, at all?"

"No, it's fine."

"And there?" he asked after changing the position of the arm.

"No, again, it's fine."

"Well I think that's about it My Lord," said Strickland inviting the Earl to get dressed, "I think you are fully recovered. If there is any recurrence, don't hesitate to get back in touch."

"That's wonderful Strickland, wonderful. I would like to reward you in some way," said the Earl.

"Don't mention it, My Lord," replied Strickland modestly. There was more than a hint of frustration in his voice, as he could not practice more of what he had once set his heart on.

"Yes I must," Lonsdale persisted, "I know – you should come to the Castle for one of our Christmas celebrations."

The private Strickland tried to be as polite as he could be whilst trying to disguise his lack of enthusiasm for the idea. "It's very kind of you My Lord but I will be probably going away for Christmas."

"Very well, in that case I have the Kaiser visiting later this month – I will be having a few guests round to shoot and dine with him; you must join us then."

"The Kaiser?" asked the surprised Strickland.

"Yes, Willie's a good friend of mine – met him a few years ago. You must come."

Strickland would be lying to himself if he said he wasn't intrigued by the offer, and struggled to come up with an excuse not to attend. Rather than discuss the matter further, however, Alex recognised his opportunity to bring the appointment to an end, and said non-committedly "I'm sure that will be most interesting, My Lord, thank you."

As he wished the Earl good morning, Alex Strickland smiled to himself at the thought of him encountering the Emperor of Germany. Never truly believing it would ever come to pass, he put the tentative offer to the back of his mind and went about his business.

A Slight Change of Plans

Mrs. Wheeler carried a pile of freshly ironed laundry to the upper floor of her residence on Abbey Street. She paused on the landing outside the door of the sitting room of her lodger and listened to his playing of Beethoven's Moonlight Sonata. The graceful melody brought a smile to her face and courteously, she waited until the beautiful notes meandered and evaporated into the ether. She knocked and entered.

"That was beautiful, Mr. Armstrong."

Cornelius looked up, slightly embarrassed by the compliment. "Thank you Mrs. Wheeler, I'm pleased I didn't know you were there – had I done so, it would have probably sounded more like *Boiled Beef and Carrots* than Beethoven." The two laughed at his characteristically self-deprecating comment.

"I've done your laundry, sir," said the housekeeper, laying the bundle of clothes on the small two-seater, "I think that is you about set?"

"Yes, I will be leaving on the nine-eighteen tomorrow. Thank you again, Mrs. Wheeler."

"Don't mention it, sir," said the housekeeper turning to leave, "I hope you enjoy your break – and very well earned, if you don't mind me saying."

As the leaves fell and the colours changed, Cornelius was preparing to exchange his notepad and detective skills for the solitude of an autumn break. He had hired a little cottage in the hamlet of Sandwick in the north Lakeland valley of Martindale for the week, and was looking forward to his break enormously: relaxation through walking, bird watching and reading would replace detective work in the grimy pubs and back alleys of Carlisle.

All that remained to do the following morning was to pop in and see Chief Constable Henry Baker, who had asked to see him before he left, and that was him for the week. *Heaven*. He packed the remainder of his clothes into his carpet bag, made sure he had his field glasses, small pocket telescope and a few books, and turned in for the night at around ten o'clock.

There was something about Mrs. Wheeler's breakfasts: the lightly browned toast, the perfectly boiled eggs, and the crispy bacon that set the ordinary weekend up nicely. The following morning, Cornelius enjoyed them all the more knowing that it was the perfect lead in to his holiday.

Two months earlier, he had been forced to cancel a similar trip when his Chief Constable, Henry Baker, had asked him to take over a case from his junior colleague, Inspector John Robinson. Robinson had been struggling for some time with an investigation into what he believed was a case of a solicitor's clerk embezzling funds from his employer. Baker finally lost patience with the younger Inspector during one of their meetings, when the latter foolishly suggested that the solicitor himself may even be involved in the defrauding of company funds.

Baker was furious with Robinson who he believed was simply clutching at various straws in an effort to force a breakthrough. In a desperate effort to salvage the investigation, Baker asked Cornelius to cancel his leave and take charge of the investigation. Armstrong acquiesced under protest and reviewed Robinson's information. He quickly established that the clerk was not actually embezzling his employer, but was actually blackmailing one of the firm's female clients, who had become embroiled in an indiscreet liaison with an entertainer from Algie's Circus, behind the back of her extremely wealthy husband.

The case proved a success for Armstrong, but he could not stop the local press having a field day with the whole sordid affair. The unfortunate woman could do nothing to keep her indiscretions out of the newspapers; her husband and the innocent solicitor were humiliated by association, and the local constabulary were pilloried for their original efforts to solve what should have been a straightforward case.

Whereas Armstrong didn't pay much attention to the press, the embarrassment of Baker was palpable, while one of his Inspectors, John Robinson, shared the wronged husband's humiliation by being relieved of the case by his senior colleague.

Armstrong's feelings of chagrin, however, revolved around his losing the opportunity to take a well-earned break. Now two-months on, this was his time to make up for missing out. His jovial mood was destined to be somewhat blunted however when he called into the station to see his superior.

"Ah, Cornelius!" said Baker as the Inspector entered his office, and then looking at the bags Armstrong was holding, "all ready to go I see."

"Morning Henry, yes I'm just off to the station now. You sent a message round to say you wanted to see me before I left."

"Yes that's right." Baker was working a thumb-full of tobacco into his pipe. He stopped, reached into his inside pocket, and drew out a white envelope. "I received this invitation earlier this week from Lord Lonsdale to join him at Lowther Castle for a few days; you know the sort of thing – shooting, wining, dining etcetera." He handed the envelope to Armstrong and resumed loading his pipe.

"Very nice," said Armstrong, uncertain what this had to do with him.

"You see the occasion?" Baker was now in a cloud of blue smoke as he waved his match in the air, partly to extinguish the flame on the end of it, and partly as an indication to Armstrong to check the contents of the envelope.

Cornelius read aloud, "'*On the occasion of the visit of His Majesty, The German Emperor, Kaiser Wilhelm II to Lowther, I would like you to join me...*' Very nice," he interrupted himself, "good for you Henry." Armstrong was impressed, but still unsure why Baker was sharing this information with him.

"I met His Lordship a few times at various events over the years, and he is gathering a few people together to share in the Kaiser's visit."

Armstrong looked at the letter again and noted the names of some of the other invitees: Sir Antony Fellows, Sir Evelyn Whatmore QC, Tristan Urquhart-Brown, Doctor Alex Strickland, Doctor Gideon Rogers. *Seems like a bunch of ordinary lads,* thought Armstrong. "Very good," he said again, handing the letter back to Baker, "nice to see you're going up in the world, Henry. Was that all?" he asked, picking his bags up again, as if to leave.

"Wait a minute, Cornelius – I didn't ask you round to boast about my social calendar. His Lordship called me yesterday to inform me that the Kaiser was interested in the work of his guests and asked if we could come prepared with stories to regale His Majesty; that's when I had a brainwave! Knowing that my best Inspector isn't a million miles away himself, I thought how useful it would be for you to pop along and join us for dinner one night."

"*Me?*"

"Yes, it would be wonderful to have you there – His Lordship was delighted when I made the suggestion."

Baker heard Armstrong mumble something under his breath, but could only make out the words "…His Lordship…" as part of some presumably derogatory comment.

"What was that?" he asked.

Cornelius ignored the question. "Oh come on Henry, *be fair!* My idea was to get away from it all and enjoy the solitude; not to get involved in some royal visit!"

"You won't be on official duty; and besides, how often do you get the chance of meeting a King?"

"Well, to be honest, I've never had the chance to meet a King, and to be even more honest, I've never really wanted the chance. I'm sure you'll enjoy it Henry, but leave me out, please."

"No, it's decided Cornelius, I've already promised His Lordship," said Baker, with a dismissive wave of his pipe-stem.

"But you asked me to cancel my last week off in July to solve the Patterson case." Armstrong was starting to sound like a spoilt child unable to get his own way.

His latest protestation simply gave Baker further encouragement, "Of course!" he cried, "that's an excellent example of your work, Cornelius; ideal to impress the Kaiser."

It was clear to the Inspector that his superior was not prepared to let him wriggle out. Armstrong, therefore, clutched at his final, feeble straw.

"How will I get to Lowther anyway? I've no transport."

"Hugh will send one of his motor vehicles for you - just give me the address and I'll make sure his chauffeur picks you up."

Game over.

With a deep sigh, Cornelius wrote down the name of the cottage - hoping it would be so remote that the chauffeur wouldn't be able to find it - and bid his superior farewell.

"Have a lovely time Cornelius," shouted Baker, as he watched his man leave.

"Thanks Henry," returned the Inspector, and then under his breath, "some chance of that."

Martindale

Cornelius put the conversation with his superior to the back of his mind, so intent was he to let the numberless, unnamed days of his holiday pass in blissful isolation.

On his first afternoon, there was more than a touch of warmth in the autumn sunshine, and he sat out on the banks of Ullswater, lazing until he watched the sun disappear over Hart Side on the other side of the lake. Planning the week ahead as he sat there, he decided that he would at some point ascend Bea Head, and if that went well, he would take the ferry across the lake and try Gowbarrow Fell or maybe even Helvellyn.

On his walk back to his tiny hide-away that afternoon, he passed the old Church of St Martin. Having read up on the area beforehand, he noted that the church had existed since the thirteenth century. Keen to view the building and its interior, he was pleasantly surprised to find a service was scheduled there for the following day at ten o'clock. The noticeboard informed the reader that the church was part of the wider parish that encompassed four churches in the area and as such, St Martin only had one service per month. Cornelius decided that it would be pleasant to reflect on his good fortune and give thanks before enjoying another relaxing day in this idyllic part of the county.

Shortly after half past nine the following morning, he left his little cottage and made the short few-hundred yard journey to take his place in the meagre old church at the mouth of the valley. The austere interior consisted of simple whitewashed walls and two long pews that ran parallel to the side of the church, beckoning the eye along the centre aisle towards a humble alter at the front of the chapel.

Cornelius took his seat halfway along the aisle, and opposite sat who were undoubtedly twin sisters.So identical were they – probably in their sixties – both were slight and lean with pointed chins, and both seemed in a mixture of excitement and agitation at the presence of a stranger. They constantly whispered to one another and pointed in the visitor's direction opposite.

As Cornelius sat trying to be as inconspicuous as possible, a ruddy-faced man with wiry, greying hair and a matching unkempt beard – seemingly in his fifties – entered the church. Grasping his cloth cap tightly with both hands as he took his seat, he offered a nod and a smile to the stranger along the pew from him.

The congregation of four sat patiently until a small commotion at the entrance signaled the arrival of the Vicar. "I'm terribly sorry I'm late," said the middle aged man who seemed to be wrestling with his attire as he entered. Amid the arms and garments, Cornelius couldn't work out whether he was undressing his top clothing with view to putting on his liturgical ware, or if he was actually levering himself into his cassock as he entered. Either way, he briefly disappeared into an alcove to the right of the entrance. After more flustered noises, the Vicar emerged virtually on the stroke of ten o'clock. As the other three people in the congregation didn't seem at all amused or concerned about the Vicar's timing or demeanour, the visitor assumed that this was normal practice.

"We shall begin our celebration by singing three verses of *Onward Christian Soldiers*," said the Vicar, once in position. Cornelius felt at no point during the service did the shepherd nor his tiny flock see any irony in singing about the hundreds of Evangelists marching as to war; nor listening to a reading about the feeding of the five thousand.

After the service had finished, the Vicar addressed the two male members of his congregation. "Miss and Miss Swan have kindly put on some refreshment for our benefit if you would like to join us?"

The local sitting along from Cornelius smiled his acquiescence, the Carlisle man nodding politely, "That would be lovely," he said.

Once the five had gathered at the rear of the church, the four locals introduced themselves to the visitor: Gertrude and Gwendolyn Swan were indeed twin sisters. They had lived in the family home beside the church all of their lives, and with the passing of both parents some years earlier, the two occupied the house alone. Armstrong listened with some amusement to their narrative, as they adopted that trait so common in identical twins of apparently thinking exactly the same thing at exactly the same time which resulted in them constantly talking over one another or finishing each other's sentences. Cornelius wondered if this habit was exacerbated by the appearance of a stranger to their tiny community.

The man introduced himself as Ned Matthews, "I have my farm further down the valley from where you are staying. What brings you here then?" he asked.

Cornelius assumed nothing much happened in this part of the world without the few locals knowing all about it. "I'm just on holiday," he said in answer to the farmer's question. "I'm a policeman in Carlisle."

"Ooh a policeman!" said one Miss Swan, "How exciting!"

"A policeman!" repeated the other.

"I knew you were from Carlisle, didn't I sister?" said the first one.

"Um…yes…Carlisle…you said he was from Carlisle sister," said the second in giddy agreement.

"We don't get many visitors…"

"…to Martindale…Not many visitors…"

"Have you ever been to Carlisle?" Cornelius asked Matthews.

"*CARLISLE?*" exclaimed the farmer incredulously, "Oh, no, no…no, no, no. I would never go all the way up to Carlisle. I went to that Penrith once," he sucked the air in through his pursed lips at his recollection, "busy place, yon!" he said with a shake of the head.

Cornelius smiled, "It must be a quiet life – something to be said for that."

"I do go into Pooley Bridge every Thursday afternoon for some supplies," said Ned in an effort to make himself sound more worldly-wise, "the Postmistress there has one of them telephones."

Before long, Vicar Jonathon Sweet had to make his apologies and set off back to Pooley Bridge to conduct another service before noon. He left in the same disorganised state in which he had arrived – all flailing arms and billowing clothing.

"Mind how you go now, Vicar," shouted Ned through the open church door.

Cornelius's entertaining morning was complete when he looked past the farmer to see the Vicar getting on a bicycle to race back to Pooley.

The two remaining men also bid the ladies good morning and left the church together. Outside was yet another incongruous sight – that of Ned's mode of transport. An old, rusting motorised cart sat patiently, lilting to one side as if to suggest any overly aggressive effort to fire the engine into action would probably see at least one of the wheels drop off.

"This old beauty gets me up and down the valley alright," said the farmer with some pride. "Can I give you a lift?"

Armstrong wondered if the owner should be in possession of a licence to operate such a thing, but decided against embarking on that particular line of enquiry. "No, it'll be fine thank you. I'm hoping to do a little bit of walking today."

"Grand day for it," retorted the farmer, "just watch out for them silly buggers wid the guns."

"Guns?" Armstrong didn't understand the comment.

"The Earl has got that German bloke over at the moment, hasn't he? They're down at the shooting lodge today hunting Martindale deer; they'll kill 'em all off if they're not careful. Daft buggers!"

Cornelius had forgotten about his meeting with Baker forty-eight hours earlier when his Chief Constable had informed him of the Kaiser's visit. He wondered briefly if Baker himself might be one of the silly buggers Ned had referred to. He shook the farmer's hand and, standing well back, wished him a safe journey home.

Matthews climbed in and closed the squealing door behind him; a series of frenzied thrusts with his foot to fire the engine had the comical effect to the spectator of the would-be driver bouncing up and down in his seat – something that appeared to threaten the very infrastructure of the vehicle. Finally, after several seconds, the old truck spluttered into life and off chugged Ned Matthews down the road with a wave out of the driver's window.

For his part, Cornelius hitched up his back pack and set off walking up Arthur's Pike, after deciding to attempt the high-level circuit of the valley.

After four hours of solitude and exercise enjoyed in equal measure, he found himself stood atop The Nab, the summit of one of the horseshoe of fells surrounding the valley. For the second time that Sunday he stood and gave thanks at the wonderment that was before him: the mellow autumnal colours blended together beautifully all around, while the late afternoon sun carved blood-red clefts in the hills that then turned to black rivulets running down towards the valley floor.

Suddenly, his reverie was disturbed by the echoes of distant gunfire. Cornelius turned and picked out the small square of bright red: the roof of the shooting lodge Ned Matthews had referred to earlier. To the left of the building were a group of about twenty men, reduced to tiny black dots; with the faint plumes of smoke and the delayed popping of the guns less than a second later, the walker deduced that the group of sportsmen were still busily engaged in their day's entertainment.

Cornelius put his binoculars to his eyes to see if he could pick out the Earl, the Kaiser, or his friend Henry Baker. It was futile of course, as without the intermittent smoke and noise coming from the guns, someone on The Nab would never know anyone was there. Cornelius smiled crookedly to himself as he let down his field glasses. *Couldn't agree more Ned, lad. Silly buggers!*

As he turned away to scour the view further, Armstrong spotted another walker on the lower slopes of Rest Dodd, one of the neighbouring fells. The man was stationary, apparently watching the shooting lodge and its occupants through his field glasses as Cornelius had been doing moments earlier. Unlike the Carlisle man however, the figure continued watching for several minutes. Armstrong wondered what was so interesting and how long he had been watching before he had spotted him. He began to wave and call out but the distance between the two, coupled with the light wind which was blowing into Armstrong's face, made it impossible for the man to hear.

He then realised that the clouds were starting to thicken as the sun began to descend; the colours began to change again, from pastel shades of apricot and mauve to russet brown and bruised purple. With the winds whipping up and the temperature already beginning to plummet, Cornelius decided it was time to make his way back. He looked round again to see if he could pick out the man on the distant hillside but there was no sign.

As he started his descent over the tricky crags near the summit of The Nab, some other movement caught his eye on the neighbouring fell: a herd of red deer were scampering across the lower slopes, presumably towards their shelter for the night. "An unsuccessful day's shooting after all," mumbled Cornelius to himself with a smile.

An Unexpected Visitor

James had been having trouble with the Rolls Royce for a few days now. The engine kept threatening to cut out, and as it spluttered along the narrow road leading down into Pooley Bridge, he wondered if it was going to give up the ghost altogether. He smiled to himself at the thought of the unintended pun. He had toyed with the idea of bringing the Mercedes Benz on his errand and was now starting to regret his decision to go against his instinct.

He pressed on through the village realising it was too late now, and as he came towards a T-junction he stopped the vehicle. Heaving the large hand brake into place, and ensuring he kept enough weight on the throttle in order to keep the engine ticking over, he checked the directions he had been given: '…follow the road through the village and then turn right following the narrow road that runs along the eastern side of the lake beyond Howtown.' He looked up from the map; sure enough, there was the track referred to. Taking a deep breath and hoping the vehicle could take the punishment of the final leg of the journey, he let off the hand brake and swung the car onto the pathway.

After about five miles of bouncing along the pothole-riddled track, James braced himself for the steep twisting incline of The Hause. With this final challenge safely negotiated, the chauffer slowly started the descent into the Martindale valley. It wasn't long before he spotted a small stone cottage about five hundred yards ahead that sat unobtrusively amid the folds in the hills near the tiny hamlet of Sandwick. Wisps of smoke from the chimney gave the little place a homely appearance. *This must be the place*, he thought.

Inside the cottage, Cornelius Armstrong was tending to the open fire, while wondering how Mrs. Wheeler always seemed to build a terrific fire with such ease, unlike his several abortive attempts. Suddenly, he stopped and listened: the unmistakable sound of a motor vehicle was approaching. Cornelius instantly made an expression his Chief Constable called his 'knife in the back face.'

He had enjoyed two days in his secluded idyll and managed to put the unscheduled meeting prior to his departure with Henry Baker to the back of his mind. The cottage was perfect: leaded windows and strong stone flags underfoot; the main room was lit by discreet gas lamps, and had a large oak mantel piece that stood over an open fire, while sturdy exposed beams hung overhead. Upstairs were two small bedrooms with low sloping ceilings; both furnished with comfortable brass beds.

Having just arrived back at the cottage less than half an hour earlier after a morning walk to Howtown, he was loading the fire up with logs to warm up the small stone dwelling. He went over to the window and eased back a curtain to see the vehicle approaching. If he was in any doubt as to what purpose there was for such a visit, then he was left without any when he saw the beautifully polished silver Rolls Royce as it made its way down the narrow decline towards the cottage.

Cornelius watched as the vehicle pulled up and idled. The driver seemed to hesitate, almost wondering whether or not he should switch the engine off. It was several seconds before the engine stopped and the driver got out of the vehicle and walked towards the only door of the building. *As impressive as his automobile,* thought Armstrong: he was dressed in a predominantly yellow uniform with navy blue piping and a matching peaked cap; he wore black gauntlets and black knee high leather boots. Cornelius opened the door to find the chauffeur with an upturned arm, just about to knock.

"Mr Armstrong, sir?" asked the driver.

"Yes," said Cornelius, knowing what was coming next.

"My name is James, sir. I've been sent by Lord Lonsdale and your colleague Chief Constable Baker to take you to Lowther Castle."

"Hello James." Cornelius offered a hand to the man who he knew was in no way to blame for his misfortune, "come inside."

James removed his glove and shook the policeman's hand. "Thank you, sir."

"I must confess to being a little unprepared," said Cornelius. "If you don't mind waiting while I gather a few things together?"

"No problem, sir, His Lordship told me to tell you that he can lend you some evening wear if you haven't got any with you."

"Evening wear?" cried Cornelius. "Why would I want evening wear? I thought I was just going along for the afternoon, tell the Kaiser what he wants to hear, and then it's straight back?"

It was clear James knew more about the arrangements than Cornelius did. The embarrassed chauffeur explained, "Not exactly, sir. His Lordship and the Chief Constable told me that you will be joining them for dinner and then staying at Lowther overnight; the Countess has organised a 'Black and White Halloween Ball.' I am to return you here tomorrow morning."

What the hell is a Black and White Ball when it's at home? Resisting the temptation to share his thoughts, the most civil thing the policeman could come up with was, "Overnight?" He was incredulous.

"The Chief Constable obviously didn't tell you, sir?"

"No, the Chief Constable didn't tell me," Armstrong mumbled to himself. *Typical bloody Henry – crafty old bugger!* "I suppose if I'm staying overnight, I had better pack some more things. If you don't mind waiting, James?"

"Not at all, sir."

Within twenty minutes, Cornelius had gathered what passed for an overnight bag, grabbed his walking boots – just in case – and locked the timber front door behind him before joining the driver in the motor car. James had re-taken his seat some minutes earlier – while his passenger was preparing his bag – in case there was a problem in re-starting the engine. Fortunately there wasn't, and the automobile was ticking over nicely as Cornelius climbed into the gunmetal leather passenger seat. Although he lacked enthusiasm about the interruption to his holiday, he would have been lying if he had said that he wasn't intrigued by experiencing how the other half lived for a few hours.

"It's a beautiful motor car," he said, looking around impressively at the interior that was as elegantly finished as the exterior was striking. The whole vehicle screamed opulence.

"Yes," agreed James, clearly proud to be driving such a vehicle, "it's called a Silver Ghost."

"I thought it was a Rolls Royce," said Armstrong without facetiousness.

The chauffeur however thought he was joking, "Very clever, sir. It is a Rolls but the model is the Silver Ghost. The publication *Autocar* hailed it as 'Best car in the world' in 1907,' – James swept his open hand through mid-air as if to indicate the headline on an imaginary newspaper – "It has a side-valve, six-cylinder 7428cc engine, with a three speed transmission. She's a beauty alright," he concluded, tapping the steering wheel.

Cornelius knew absolutely nothing – and wished to know absolutely nothing – about motor vehicles, and he was pleased the driver's pride in his charge had apparently acted as a distraction to his earlier dim-witted comment. As for the gobbledygook about valves, cylinders and however many transmission speeds the damn thing had, he simply chose to smile and nod in feigned understanding in order not to dampen James's enthusiasm. Sadly for him, the chauffeur took this as encouragement to continue the technical conversation. Once the motor car was maneuvered round to commence the return journey north along the dusty track, he picked up his discarded thread once more, believing his passenger to be interested. "She's been playing up a bit lately" – and then to himself – "I wonder if one of the cylinders is playing up? I very nearly brought the Mercedes Benz the Kaiser gave to His Lordship the last time he visited."

Cornelius saw his chance to change the subject. "Speaking of the Kaiser, what's he like?"

"Difficult for me to say, sir," replied James discretely. "He has visited Lowther two or three times now and His Lordship seems to enjoy his company tremendously. I don't have a lot to do with the man myself but I've heard some of the staff grumbling about his manner and some of his entourage. You know how things are below stairs, sir."

"How many staff are employed at the castle?"

"Oh, His Lordship and Her Ladyship have a decent number, sir; there are maids, footmen, and kitchen staff. Of course the numbers have swelled still further these last couple of days as the Kaiser has brought his own staff, and the other guests have also brought a butler or a maid."

"And you, James – how long have you driven for His Lordship?"

"I've been with him for seven years now, sir; ever since he bought this beauty in 1906."

Cornelius feared that James was not only steering the vehicle, but was about to steer the conversation back towards the subject *of* the vehicle. For the remainder of the journey therefore, he made a conscious effort to talk about the weather, the scenery, anything but the damn automobile.

Lowther Castle

The journey proved an unexpectedly pleasant one for the off-duty policeman. James was amiable company and the two chatted desultorily for most of the way.

Without ever being an expert in architecture, Cornelius appreciated the style and beauty of buildings, as well as their history, and as the chauffer turned onto the long driveway of Lowther Castle on the stroke of noon, Armstrong couldn't fail to be impressed by the structure that loomed before them. After reading several books on the castles of Britain and Europe, the perfect symmetry of the crenelated turrets of the structure brought to mind the extravagant Bavarian Castles he had often wondered about.

As the Silver Ghost made its way up the tree-lined drive that was dappled with autumnal sunshine, James sensed his passenger's impressions of the castle. "The site dates back to the time of Edward I. The current castle was designed by Robert Smirke over a hundred years ago."

"Very impressive," marveled Cornelius.

James swung the car round in an arc and parked in front of a set of imposing stone steps that led to the large double doors – they were guarded on either side by two ferocious lions. As if by magic, a liveried footman – in the same immaculate yellow and navy uniform donned by the chauffer – appeared as Cornelius opened the passenger door.

"Good afternoon, sir. Welcome to Lowther Castle." He helped himself to the visitor's bags that were strapped to the exterior rack at the back of the vehicle. "My name is Michael and if there is anything you need, please don't hesitate to ask. If you would just follow me sir, I'll show you inside."

Cornelius followed the footman up the steps while James took the car down one of the graveled driveways that ran along either side of the castle, presumably back to the garage. "The Earl and his party are still out this morning sir," said Michael entering the castle, "so cook took the liberty of making you a light lunch that has been set up in your room. I hope you don't mind?"

Armstrong followed his guide into the main hall and was struck by the eclectic décor: beautiful Regency chairs, stunning paintings, a suit of armour, a large center-piece round table that was polished to within an inch of its life, ancient flags adorning another wall, alongside a stag's head. A broad sweeping staircase led away from the black and white-tiled floor of the hall to the first floor.

"Sir?" Michael stood patiently waiting for an answer.

"Oh, yes, I'm sorry," said Cornelius, embarrassed by his distraction, "that will be fine."

Michael led the way up the staircase as Cornelius looked down on several members of staff – all bedecked in the now familiar livery – scuttling back and forth across the hallway carrying out their numerous duties in preparation for the celebrations later.

The visitor was shown across a landing and down a long corridor with rooms either side. Halfway down, the footman opened a door and stood aside for Cornelius to enter. "There you go sir. I hope you find everything to your liking."

The room was a beautiful octagon shape with tasteful pale yellow wallpaper and a green, subtly patterned, carpet. A log fire burned in the stone fireplace, taking the edge off the autumnal nip, while overhead, in the centre of the moulded ceiling there hung a large gilt-and-crystal chandelier. *I wonder what the Royal accommodation is like?* wondered the man who had never experienced such opulence.

Under the window, that afforded a stunning view of the fells, stood two other fine Regency chairs and a matching table, on which was placed a ham salad, referred to by the footman as "a light lunch."

Before sitting down the welcome meal, Cornelius unpacked his small bag. Opening the wardrobe, he found an evening suit, presumably for the ball that night. Taking it out and trying on the jacket, he wasn't in the least bit surprised to find that it fit perfectly. With a shake of the head, he replaced the jacket, filled one drawer of the dresser with his own few belongings and sat down to his lunch.

As the clock struck one, and with the Earl and his party still nowhere to be seen, the visitor decided to explore the grounds of the castle, the garden of which, according to James the chauffer, had been "...designed by Thomas Mawson and inspired by the gardens at Versailles."

Armstrong didn't know anything about garden design and he had certainly never been to Versailles, but as the afternoon progressed he couldn't help but to grudgingly acknowledge that he was enjoying his trip to Lowther immensely; firstly the opulence and facilities of the castle itself, and now the stunning beauty of the grounds made it all feel like a genuine part of his holiday. *I better not admit that to Henry when I see him*, he thought to himself as he strolled along the limestone escarpment on the west side of the grounds which provided a breathtaking view across the fells to the northern mountains of the Lake District.

It was almost four o'clock by the time he had completed a full circle of the enormous estate. He returned over the south lawn that was being ornamented with marquees and through the stable courtyard that was being swept clean of the mud and slurry trailed in by the hooves of the returning horses. The Earl and his party were back.

Cornelius found his friend and superior in the large hallway talking to another, slightly built man who leaned on a stick. Henry Baker looked up when he saw his man enter. "Cornelius, how lovely to see you!"

"Hello, Henry."

"Isn't this an incredible place?" Before Armstrong could answer, the excited Chief Constable continued, "You've just missed the Earl and the Kaiser, they've gone to freshen up. But let me introduce you to another of the Earl's guests – this is Doctor Alex Strickland. Alex, this is my finest Inspector, Cornelius Armstrong."

Armstrong shook hands with the man he estimated to be at least ten years his junior, "Pleased to meet you, Alex."

"And you Cornelius, Henry has told me a lot about you. I was hoping to have a decent chat with a like-minded fellow."

Armstrong took that to mean that the younger man wasn't so enamoured with being here either.

"Why don't I leave you two to get to know each other, while I go to my room?" Henry started to climb the staircase, "If you go through to the library, I'm sure one of the staff will get you a drink."

"Typical Henry," said Cornelius, watching as his friend disappeared from view on the landing, "anyone would think he owned the place."

"I like him," said Strickland with a smile, "It's a good job he's been here the last day or two; it would have been torture otherwise."

"Yes, don't get me wrong," said the policeman, "we're good pals me and Henry – go back a long way. Shall we go and see if we can get that drink?"

As the two made their way down the hall, both men became a little embarrassed by Strickland's pronounced limp. "Sorry, I'm not the speediest of companions these days," said the Doctor, feeling the need to break the ice.

"You seem to be a young lad to have such a bad injury," said Cornelius, not particularly wishing to ignore the issue. The two entered the library where the Earl's butler was on hand to offer them a drink. "The Earl is resting, gentlemen. Can I offer you a drink?"

"A small glass of rum for me please," said Armstrong.

"That sounds very civilized," agreed Strickland before addressing the policeman's question. "Yes, I was a decent sportsman in my day, but my enthusiasm for diversity got the better of me and took me into the Army – well, the Volunteers at least. I went out to South Africa in 1900 and lost my leg for my troubles." He reached down and rubbed the joint of his prosthetic limb and his stump. "Damn thing aches when I do too much."

"I'm sorry," was the best Armstrong could come up with. He felt an element of relief when the butler placed the drinks on the occasional table that sat beside them. "Thank you."

"Oh, don't worry about it," said Strickland philosophically, "there were a lot of other blokes that weren't as lucky, I suppose."

Armstrong then had another associated thought. "I seem to remember my cousin telling me he looked after the Penrith lads at one point – can you remember Sergeant *George* Armstrong?"

"George!" exclaimed the Doctor, enthusiastically. "He's your cousin? Good heavens, what a small world! Yes George *was* our Sergeant out there – he was a great bloke. Because I had to leave early I lost touch with him and most of the lads; they stayed on and, following my recuperation, I completed my medical studies and took over my father's practice in town. Good heavens, dear old George."

"Me and George are good pals," said Cornelius, "whenever he's home we spend as much time together as we can. He recently came back with the regiment from the subcontinent. Maybe I could put you in touch with him again?"

"What a smashing idea," said Alex, and then after some thought and downing his drink, "but first things first I suppose – let's get this damn thing over with."

The Halloween Ball

Lady Grace Cecile Gordon married Hugh Lowther in June 1878. When he became Earl with the death of his father, she became the Countess of Lonsdale and would prove herself hard-working and popular amongst the staff and locals. She liked nothing better than to host the great and the good, and given that the Kaiser's stay at Lowther coincided with Halloween, she insisted on holding a black and white ball to commemorate the occasion.

The Earl and Countess's guests would enjoy dinner before being joined by local villagers afterwards, as His Majesty had expressed an interest in meeting some of the ordinary people of Cumberland during his visit. Everyone was to dress in black and white, and Halloween masks were optional.

As Cornelius Armstrong descended the stairs shortly after six thirty – as per Thomas's instruction – he was struck by the amazing effect of the decoration throughout the hallway and the wide corridor leading through to the dining room: black and white banners hung from the ceilings while beautiful contrasting ostrich feathers protruded from large pots that stood on the black and while tiled floor. A string quintet, seated to the right of the main entrance, were playing a piece by Brahms.

The guests were due to line up along the corridor in order to be presented to the Kaiser at a quarter to seven before following the Royal party into the dining room for a prompt seven o'clock serving. As the others gradually joined Armstrong in the line, he exchanged a nod with Alex Strickland. As the hour approached, increased fidgeting and mumbling amongst those lined up signified a rise in the level of excitement.

Finally, as the clock in the hall struck seven, the Royal party – consisting of the Earl and Countess, the Kaiser, some military officers and diplomats, and several Prussian aristocrats – appeared from the adjacent drawing room.

The Earl was in white tie and tails, like the other gentlemen, while the Countess wore an elegant silk gown – naturally halved in black and white – and two matching feathers which were attached to her elaborate headpiece. The Kaiser was in a white military uniform, weighed down with medals. The only splashes of colour came from the German officers who wore their red tunics and blue sashes – like their King, their left breasts were covered with decorations.

The party stopped before being presented to the guests, as the musicians played the British national anthem, followed by *Deutschland Uber Alles*. The Earl then invited the Kaiser forward and proceeded to introduce him to the guests he knew, while relying on those he did not to introduce themselves.

"Cornelius Armstrong, My Lord; Your Majesty," said the policeman with a nod to both men, when his turn came. After a slight pause he felt obliged to explain, "I am a policeman from Carlisle." With no response from either man, he decided to elaborate, "I work for Chief Constable Henry Baker who asked me to come along for this evening's celebration."

"Ah yes, Henry," said the Earl evenly. The Kaiser showed no expression or recognition, although he did seem to pause momentarily and study the horns of Armstrong's moustache with some envy. He and the Earl then moved on to Sir Antony Fellows, who was standing next to the policeman. The rest of the entourage seemed even less interested in the Inspector than Lowther and Wilhelm. After several minutes of inane handshaking – and despite Baker's original explanation – Cornelius was now beginning to wonder what the purpose of his presence was.

As the party processed into the dining room, those in the line broke ranks and began to follow. Cornelius again caught the eye of Alex who wore a similar lackluster expression; it seemed that both men were anticipating a mixture of predicted boredom with unpredicted boredom.

Fifty guests took their seats, introduced themselves to those close by, and began the desultory conversations that accompany such an occasion.

On one side, Armstrong found himself sitting next to Sir Antony who moved in the same sporting circles as the Earl, whilst on the other was the wife of Lowther's physician, Gideon Rogers. She wore a black jacket over a white lace blouse and had a smart little straw hat on her head with a white veil twisted around it. Armstrong felt Mrs. Rogers appeared considerably younger than her husband who was seated further up the long table, that was decorated with napkins splayed like peacock's tails, and three-armed silver candelabras, positioned perfectly like sentinels down the centre, from which burned cinnamon-scented candles that gave the room a pleasing aroma.

Directly opposite the policeman was a polar explorer called Eric Franklin who had accompanied Shackleton on his Nimrod Expedition to Antarctica five years earlier. Beside Franklin was Alex Strickland and on the other side of *him* sat a German diplomat who introduced himself as Heinz-Harold Fleischer.

It quickly became apparent that the diplomat had strong opinions, and Armstrong felt he would never die wondering what would happen if he didn't express them. As one of the staff ladled soup from an ornate tureen, the subject of Franklin's polar adventure was raised. Mrs. Rogers was in the process of asking a question of the explorer when Fleischer interrupted, leaning over Doctor Strickland as he did so, "It is a great pity zat zi Norwegians beat your Captain Scott to zi pole is it not?"

Armstrong sensed that the loss of Scott was felt deeply by the exploration fraternity but was impressed that Franklin didn't rise to the bait. Instead, he demonstrated admirable diplomacy himself by speaking at some length about the hazards of such a journey, and concluded by paying due regard to both British and Norwegian expeditions.

"Very sad," concluded Fleischer, seemingly determined to have the last word.

The rather tense atmosphere was relieved somewhat when the staff moved forward to clear the table and serve the main course of venison. As the chinking of silver cutlery on china competed with the several conversations that were taking place up and down the table, Alex Strickland peered between the tentacles of one of the candelabras and raised the subject of his proposed meeting with the Armstrong cousins. "Cornelius, I've been thinking about us getting together with George. How about if you come back to my house tomorrow and George can come down on the train and join us for dinner."

"How will I get back to Martindale?" asked the policeman.

"Well if George doesn't mind, he can take you back in my father's car; he can then stay with you and bring the car back to Penrith the following day before returning to Carlisle."

Cornelius laughed, "You really have got it all calculated haven't you?"

"What do you think?"

It seemed as though Strickland's idea was the only thing that could cheer him up this evening; besides, Armstrong would never pass up the chance of spending some time with his cousin. "I'm sure George would like that," he said.

"I'm sure the Earl won't mind me using his telephone. I will contact the regiment in the morning and see if I can get a message to him."

"Regiment?" questioned the explorer beside Strickland, "Am I to assume there is an army connection?"

"Yes," said the Doctor, "it turns out that Cornelius is the cousin of my Sergeant during the South African War."

"Ah, zi war with zi Dutch-men, Herr Doctor! Were you zere?" interjected Fleischer.

Clearly piqued by the interruption, and apparently losing patience with his dining partner, Alex slowly turned back to his dish, "Yes," he said quietly.

"Again, sadly not your country's finest hour," persisted the German.

Strickland felt the blood coursing through his veins. "Well your government made sure of that didn't they?" he said to his plate, trying to keep his composure.

"You are surely mistaken Herr Doctor," replied the diplomat calmly, "Germany tried to help the peace process."

"By supplying arms to the Boers?" Strickland snapped, much to the shock of those within earshot. The sudden silence rippled up the table, prompting everyone to look in the direction of the source.

The silence was broken by Fleischer, who twitched with satisfaction beneath his gaudy whiskers. 'Your understanding of our foreign policy needs improving, old man."

Strickland waited for the embarrassed table to resume its various conversations before replying. "Really, *old man*? I seem to recall the Germany's misreading of the *Entente Cordiale* with France in 1904, and then our similar arrangement with Russia in 1907. Then there was the *Daily Telegraph* affair a year later; hardly examples of rigorous foreign policy making, or sensible leadership for that matter." He looked down the table in the general direction of the Kaiser.

"Simply misunderstandings," was the diplomat's infuriating reply. "Whereas you British in zi Cape – how you say – you were land grabbing."

"It seems to me Germany's ambitions weren't so dissimilar," retorted the young Doctor, "as the Boxer Rebellion in China demonstrates. What did the Kaiser say as he sent his expedition? 'Prisoners will not be taken'."

"Whereas your treatment of Boer woman and children I seem to remember was commendable," countered Fleischer, sarcastically, "first burn zeir farms and zen house zem in – what was it again? Ah yes, zat is right – zi concentration camps, I sink.

"Germany is a peaceful country," he continued, and then, indicating up the table, "you only have to look at His Majesty and zi Earl, zey get on like – how you say – zi burning house."

Strickland's face began to redden, his little inner voice of reason was momentarily silenced by a surge of emotions: hurt, fury, and a thirst for retribution concerning his personal loss. He spun round to face the man on his left for the first time, but noting that he had become the centre of attention, he regained his composure and turned back to his meal.

Armstrong felt most of the immediate company shared his view of Fleischer – he was a boorish oaf who seemed to enjoy provoking his fellow guests by expressing his extreme opinions and using stupid terms like 'how you say' and 'old man.' The German continued his annoying behaviour until Thomas, the butler, announced, "Your Majesty, My

Lord, if you would permit? The ladies should now be excused to the drawing room while the gentlemen will be served port and brandy."

Everyone stood to allow the ladies to leave before the uncorking of a port bottle, with a loud *thwipp*, was the signal for the gentlemen to spread out and relax. Cornelius wasted no time in steering Strickland away from Fleischer and moving him towards one of the leather armchairs that had been brought in for the comfort of the Earl's male guests.

Curious Liaisons

While the decorated halls and rooms of Lowther Castle screamed elegance and opulence, the castle's underbelly was basic and functional as befitted the servants' working environment. On the night of the Halloween ball, it was a hive of activity as scores of staff scurried back and forth along the narrow corridors, bobbing and swerving around one another in order to satisfy their masters and mistresses above stairs.

The Earl and Countess's staff had been supplemented by those of their guests; and a combination of the temporary staff's unfamiliarity of their surroundings and the sheer numbers of staff created a hot, uncomfortable environment that was alive with sound and fraught with tension.

It was the job of the Earl's butler, Thomas, and the housekeeper, Mrs. Lewis, to keep order and momentum, especially on a night like this where everything had to run with military precision.

At half past eight, once the dessert dishes had been removed and the ladies had adjourned to the drawing room, the staff knew that they were entering the final phase of their packed programme of duties.

While the Earl and his guests enjoyed their brandy and cigars, the anxiety eased palpably in the servants' hall and, inevitably, some of the staff began tittle-tattling about the evening's events and the characters whom they had encountered. As one of the Earl's valets was trying to impress one of the lady's maids with his knowledge of the Royal Families of Europe, another spoke over him with his witnessing of the verbal spat between Strickland and Fleischer.

"That was a queer to do with the Penrith Doctor and that German with the whiskers," he said, with all the smugness of a knowledgeable gossip.

Instinctively, everyone within earshot turned to look at Violet, Strickland's maid who was sitting at the long servants' table. She had also witnessed the argument, as had Emily, Lady Rodgers's maid. Violet reddened with embarrassment. She had struck up a friendship with Emily in the few days that they had been at the castle. They had helped each other in trying to remember the contents of each little storeroom drawer and cupboard, and what jams, pickles or preserves were to be served when and with what. Emily put her hand on her young friend's arm in comfort.

Violet's blushes were spared when one of the bells in the row above the door began to ring: it was a summons from the dining room.

Thomas appeared as if by magic, "Come along, chop chop," he announced to everyone with a clap of his hands, "we are required once more."

Above stairs, one of the Earl's guests had spotted a tiny light in the distant blackness of the grounds. "My Lord, what is that?"

His comment led to all those present walking across to the window to see the subject of his question.

"Ah, it is our other guests, gentlemen," said the Earl. He tugged on the sash of the bell- pull that hung by the fireplace in order to summon the servants, before leading his guests out onto the front steps of the castle where they were joined by the ladies.

The guests watched as the tiny orange speck of light grew in size and gradually began forming into a line. It became apparent that the line of light was in fact hundreds of villagers who were marching up the long drive with open torches toward the castle. It was an amazing sight on this clear black night.

The spectators had been there for a matter of seconds before servants appeared with coats and shawls, while the outdoor staff started lighting the lanterns which were positioned throughout the grounds and gardens. Those on the terrace watched until the villagers processed through the inner gates of the castle, and then Lord Lonsdale announced, "Welcome to Lowther, everyone! Please make your way round to the South Lawn and enjoy the festivities."

No sooner had the words left his lips than the perfectly choreographed evening continued with a firework exploding into the night sky. There was a gasp of approval from those on the terrace, and a cheer from the villagers who were joining them on this special occasion.

"I think I might turn in for an early night, Cornelius." Alex Strickland placed a hand on the policeman's shoulder and turned to go back inside.

"Are you alright Alex?" asked Armstrong.

"Yes, I'll be fine. I'll see you in the morning."

"Goodnight."

Cornelius watched the young man walk away as the excitement grew among those who remained. Having toured the grounds and gardens earlier in the day, and knowing that the majority of the guests would follow the Earl's direction to the South Lawn at the rear of the castle, he decided to seek a little peace and quiet by the Countess's Garden on the west side of the grounds. He discretely held back while most people followed the line around the east side of the castle before ambling in the other direction.

With the temperature dropping to freezing point, Cornelius muffled his coat up tight and remembered a bench that sat on the porch of the Countess's Summer House facing her garden. It proved to be a perfectly secluded spot from where he could sit quietly looking at the stars.

Having read a book recently on astronomy, the policeman wondered if he could recall the various constellations. After ten minutes of marvelling at the wonders of the universe, he picked out Orion's belt and the bright star above it and slightly to the left – *beetle-something-or-other.*

His reverie was broken by the sound of distance voices. Peering through the blackness, he made out three figures about fifty or sixty yards to his left. Looking closer, he saw that one was a man in evening wear – his white collar being visible above his long overcoat while his patent leather shoes glistened in the darkness. Squinting further from his concealed position, Armstrong suddenly realised it was Fleischer, the obnoxious diplomat he had met earlier.

What made the scene so incongruous was the fact that he appeared to be talking to two modestly dressed companions – presumably two of the villagers who had joined the celebrations. From what he could make out, they appeared to be a man and a woman, quite a bit younger than the German, although he couldn't be sure.

Why would he be talking to them?

It was clear that it wasn't a chance meeting as the three were in animated conversation for several minutes. Frustrated at not being able to hear exactly what was said, Cornelius had to rely on the low temperature which indicated who was speaking at any one time, as their breath could be clearly seen in the cold night air.

As the three ended their conversation, they dispersed, with Fleischer heading back towards the South Lawn while his two confidantes turned and headed back through the Countess's Garden towards the main the gates of the castle – presumably they were leaving.

Cornelius leaned further back into the shadows of the porch and held his breath and the two passed within twenty feet of him. He saw enough of them to confirm that they were considerably younger than the diplomat, and fortunately – so engrossed were they in their hissed conversation – they never suspected they were being watched.

Waiting until they were out of sight and earshot, the policeman left his hiding place and headed after Fleischer. Linking the Countess's Garden with the fountain behind it was a natural tunnel of overhanging trees, from which the staff had hung hollowed-out pumpkins. The illuminated faces snarled and grimaced at Armstrong as he saw the distant silhouette of Fleischer turn left at the end of the long pathway, walking back towards the South Lawn.

The policeman followed his footsteps and re-joined the main body of merry-makers.

Fireworks exploded high overhead, leaving smoky trails across the night sky and a drifting scent of burned excitement in the air. Many guests wore masks while jugglers, musicians, harlequins and acrobats contributed to the confused amusement. The Earl's head chef was manning a spit on which a large hog roasted, in order to feed the villagers.

Armstrong eased his way through the crowd, scanning this way and that. Fleischer was nowhere to be seen. Standing in the centre of the lawn, pondering the strange events of the evening, a voice came from behind, "Enjoying yourself, Inspector?"

"Hello Henry," said Cornelius, turning to see his Chief Constable grinning at him. "I think I've got a bone to pick with you haven't I?"

Baker's expression invited an explanation.

"You said the Kaiser wanted me to tell him about some interesting cases. I haven't spoken to him!"

"Well, there's a lot to occupy him and a lot of people with stories to tell."

"Oh I see – so I was dragged along just in case he got bored?"

"Come along Cornelius, tell me you're not interested in seeing how the other half live?"

"Well, I suppose there are a few interesting characters here," conceded the Inspector, looking around at the noisy revelers who covered the South Lawn.

"Yes, talking about interesting characters," said Henry, "what was that carry on earlier with young Strickland?"

Armstrong explained the background to the heated outburst over the dinner table. "That German bloke was a bit of a prig but Alex seemed to fly off the handle with very little provocation."

Henry recalled a conversation he had had with Strickland earlier that morning, "Yes I had a chat with him when we were out hunting. It left me in no doubt he didn't have much time for our German visitors."

"I'm going back to Penrith with him tomorrow. It turns out he knows my cousin George – they served together in South Africa."

"He told me that's where he lost his leg," interrupted Baker.

"George is meeting us for something to eat at Alex's house." Armstrong then changed the subject to that of Strickland's antagonist. "What do you *know* about the German, Fleischer?"

"Not very much, I haven't had anything to do with him. I don't think he came hunting this morning, and come to think of it, he wasn't there yesterday either."

Armstrong nodded thoughtfully as he remembered seeing the hunting party in Martindale. "I saw him twenty minutes ago talking to two of the villagers, which I thought was a little odd. I was looking for him when you came over.

Henry smiled at his subordinate, "I sense your curiosity is aroused Inspector – you *are* enjoying yourself after all!"

A Busman's Holiday

Alex Strickland spent a fitful night staggering between hazy remembrance and maudlin self-pity, tormented as he was by his encounter with Fleischer and the thought of all he represented: a bunch of stuck-up, self-important bullies, forever sticking those noses into other countries' affairs. Not until the autumnal dawn crept through the wooden slats of the shutters did Strickland fall asleep.

Further along the landing, Cornelius Armstrong also lay awake for much of the night, pondering the evening's events. *What was Fleischer up to? And who were those two people he was talking to?*

Cornelius had heard from Henry Baker that the Earl's chauffer would not be available until after lunch the following day to take him and Strickland back to Penrith; so the policeman decided to walk to the nearby village to see if his curiosity regarding the German's two companions could be satisfied.

He descended the stairs shortly after half past eight, and entering the dining room he saw his superior officer in the process of decapitating his boiled egg.

"Morning Henry."

"Ah, Cornelius, good morning. Please sit down." Baker nodded at the vacant seat opposite while continuing to struggle with his egg. "Sleep well?"

"Yes, not too bad thanks," lied Cornelius.

No sooner had he sat down when one of the staff appeared at his side to take his order. He asked for some scrambled eggs on toast and a pot of tea before resuming his conversation.

"I'm thinking about having a walk into the village this morning."

Baker smiled, "Never off duty eh, Inspector?"

"Well it would kill a little time," offered Armstrong by way of a defence, "I'm just interested in some of the characters for the ball last night."

"The German and his two friends in particular no doubt?"

Cornelius shrugged, allowing Henry his fun. "Have you seen anything of Alex this morning?" he asked.

"No," replied Baker, "mind you, there's not many people who have surfaced yet," he added, glancing round the room that consisted of Dr and Mrs. Rogers, and two of the Kaiser's military staff who seemed oblivious to the others present, such was the intensity of their conversation.

Once Armstrong had finished his breakfast, he left Baker to return to his room to change into his walking boots. Coming down the stairs, as he was going up, was the young Doctor from Penrith.

"Good morning Alex, is everything all right?"

"Morning Cornelius, yes fine thanks."

Armstrong thought he looked a little pale and drawn, "Did you sleep alright?"

"Not terribly well I'm afraid. You?"

"Not too bad thanks. I was going to have a little walk into the village if you fancy coming?"

"No, you go on, Cornelius. I'll have some breakfast and then try and contact George at the castle about coming to Penrith tonight. I'll speak to you when you get back and hopefully we can then get out of this dreadful place." His head oscillated from side to side with this final comment.

"As you wish. I'll see you later."

The two went in opposite directions and, twenty minutes later, the off-duty policeman was striding down the driveway of Lowther Castle, heading towards the nearby village of Askham.

In the policeman's experience – whether he was in the largest metropolis or the tiniest settlement – there was one establishment that would invariably provide the investigator with his greatest source of information: the local pub.

It was mid-morning by the time he found himself standing in front of Askham's hostelry peering through the window, having found the door locked. Inside, the publican was tidying his establishment preparing for business later that day. The light tapping on the window attracted his attention. Looking up he saw a well-turned-out man; not someone he recognised from the village.

"We're closed, sir," he shouted.

Outside, Cornelius Armstrong cupped his hands round his mouth, "I'm sorry to disturb you, but could I have a little of your time?" and then by way of an explanation, believing it would probably gain him access, "I am a policeman, staying up at the castle."

The publican nodded and motioned the stranger towards the door.

Once it was open, the Carlisle man completed his introduction, "Thank you for your time, and apologies again for disturbing you. My name is Inspector Cornelius Armstrong," he said offering a hand.

"John Bowler," replied the publican, "please come in."

"I wonder if you were at the ball last night?" asked Cornelius, not wanting to waste either his time, or that of his host.

"Of course," replied Bowler, "the whole village was there. It was a great night, and very kind of the Earl and the Countess – quite a thrill to see the Kaiser as well, if I'm honest. Everyone seemed to have a good time."

"Did you know all of the people there?"

Bowler thought for a while, "Yes I think so." Before Armstrong asked his next question, he added, "the only two people who weren't from the village were the young Irish couple who have been staying here the last couple of nights."

The policeman's eyes lit up, "Irish couple?" His instinct told him that they had to be the two speaking to Fleischer the previous evening. "Are they still here?" he asked.

"You've just missed them," said the publican, "they left less than an hour ago."

Armstrong exhaled heavily through the nose. "Did they say what they were doing here?"

"Yes, they were newlyweds – they were on honeymoon."

This rather stumped Cornelius; were they the same couple he saw at the castle? If it were a different couple, then who were *they* and where were *they* staying? And regardless of who they were, what was Fleischer up to?

"Thank you Mr Bowler," he said shaking hands again, "and apologies again for disturbing you."

"No problem, Inspector," said Bowler, a little bemused by the whole encounter, "enjoy the rest of your stay at the castle."

Oblivious to the pleasant morning, Cornelius wandered absentmindedly back towards the castle, mulling over the characters and the events he had witnessed during the previous day. *Ireland, why always Ireland?*

A thought then occurred to him: for the past three years, the newspapers had been full of 'the Irish problem' and the seemingly constant threat of civil war as the Home Rule debate raged on. More than one report had suggested arms were being smuggled into Ulster by Unionists and Nationalists, and Germany had cropped up as being one of the sources.

Could it be that the two were working with Fleischer to arrange the smuggling of arms? All seems a bit far-fetched. And besides, why would the Germans use the Kaiser's visit as a front for such an operation? Unless the Kaiser knows nothing about it, of course.

"Cornelius!"

Wandering up the drive, the policeman's thoughts were disturbed by Strickland, who was calling, and awkwardly hopping down the wide shallow steps towards Armstrong.

"Cornelius! I managed to get through to George earlier – it was wonderful to hear his voice again after so long." The sight of the Doctor hurrying towards the policeman in a kind of run-cum-skip, by swinging his prosthetic leg, was a little uncomfortable for his new friend, but Strickland's excitement clearly negated any inhibitions he had concerning his disability.

"Even better, he can join us for dinner later. He will arrive in Penrith around five o'clock and then he can drive you back to Martindale tonight. He will then return my father's car to Penrith and return to Carlisle at lunchtime tomorrow."

"That's great news," said Armstrong, as the two walked back towards the steps "it'll be nice for you to meet up again after so long."

As soon as they entered the front door they encountered Chief Constable Henry Baker who looked far from the relaxed holiday-maker Armstrong had left earlier that morning.

"Ah, Cornelius, thank goodness you're back – something very disturbing has happened." He turned to Strickland, "Alex could you excuse us?"

"Certainly," said the Doctor heading towards the stairs, "I'll see you later Cornelius."

Once Strickland started to walk away, Baker motioned his Inspector towards the drawing room, "We need to speak with you urgently."

"We?"

Baker opened the door. It was the first time Cornelius had been in the drawing room: it boasted the same opulence as the rest of the house, with paintings and friezes giving the room a certain elegance. In front of the open fire lay the skin of a once magnificent tiger, whose head snarled at those present as if in its death defiance. Sitting in the Queen Ann armchairs on either side were Lord Lonsdale and the Kaiser, with the King's equerry standing behind His Majesty.

After re-introducing his Inspector to the illustrious trio, he explained his concerns to his subordinate, "Inspector, this was found in the hallway this morning." He handed a piece of paper to Armstrong.

On it were words apparently cut from a newspaper which read:

The Kaiser is a criminal
The only good German is a dead German
The King must die

Concerns and Suspicions

Cornelius Armstrong looked at the paper and instinctively squeezed one of the horns of his moustache. Not waiting to be given permission, he absentmindedly sat down on a settee that matched the beautiful chairs which the Earl and his guest occupied.

"What do you make of it Inspector?" Chief Constable Baker felt the need to break the silence. "How serious do you think it is?"

Armstrong looked from the Kaiser to the Earl and back again.

"I think it is in everyone's interest that you speak candidly Inspector," said Hugh Lowther, apparently believing the policeman's hesitation was based on his wish not to offend.

Suitably re-assured, Armstrong shared his initial thoughts. "Well given the number of people who have been in the castle during the last couple of days, it could be from any number of people."

"Are you suggesting His Majesty has a number of enemies here?" The Kaiser's equerry Von Gerber's tone was clipped and haughty.

"I'm not suggesting anything sir," replied the policeman, "but the fact is that scores of people have been here recently, some of whom are not known to any of us. We cannot be certain someone didn't take advantage of the Countess's generosity last night and use the ball to make this threat."

"Do you think it is serious?" asked the Earl.

"I'm afraid we must treat it as such, My Lord. A lot of work has been done, first to wade through a newspaper to find certain words, and then to cut them out and stick them to the paper.

"If it was an idle prank, it would have been easier for someone to scribble the note and leave it lying around somewhere. With the great number of people coming and going, it would have been almost impossible to identify the handwriting on such a note."

After leaving a suitable pause to let his views sink in, the Inspector asked, "May I ask what Your Majesty's schedule is between now and your return to Germany?"

Von Gerber replied on Wilhelm's behalf, "His Majesty will continue to hunt with Lord Lonsdale and tour the surrounding areas; he will then attend a farewell dinner given in his honour by the Lord Lieutenant of Cumberland on Thursday. The royal party then leaves on Friday morning."

"Is this widely known?"

"I believe the programme over events and whereabouts were published in the local press before the King arrived," said the Earl.

"I think this itinerary should be changed." Armstrong's tone suggested he wasn't intending to debate the matter.

"Is that really necessary?" asked the equerry.

"I think it is," said the Inspector firmly. "There is probably nothing in this but I don't see the need to take unnecessary risks. I saw you all hunting the other day at the lodge in Martindale; there was a man further down the hill from me also watching you. Again, he could have been a completely innocent spectator, but then again…" he let the thought hang in the air. "Whatsmore, with guns to hand and shooting to be done, coupled with the fact that any would-be assassin may well know the King's whereabouts, why take the chance?"

It was the first time anyone had used the word 'assassin' and it seemed to give the issue a sharp focus. The Kaiser nodded curtly to Von Gerber.

"Very well," said the equerry.

"I agree," said Lowther "but it will be difficult to cancel the gala dinner."

"Where is it taking place?" asked the Inspector.

"At the Brantwood Hotel at Stainton."

"On Thursday?"

"Yes."

"Could I suggest a change of venue, My Lord, just to be on the safe side?"

"That's a good idea, I will arrange it immediately."

"And it might be a good idea not to make the new venue known to anyone who does not need to know," instructed Armstrong. The Earl nodded. The policeman then turned to the Kaiser, "I suggest Your Majesty enjoys the luxury of the castle for the next few days until Thursday; I'm sure your military staff can give you adequate protection for the remainder of your visit."

"Thank you for your help, Inspector," said the Earl, apparently dismissing the policeman.

"Thank you again Cornelius," echoed Henry Baker.

"If I may before I leave," ventured Armstrong looking at Von Gerber, "where is your colleague Fleischer this morning?"

"Herr Fleischer had to return urgently to Berlin this morning," replied the equerry.

All present looked quizzically at the Carlisle policeman, who stared into the middle distance, nodding slowly and tweaking his moustache.

"Thank you," he said at last. "And thank you for your hospitality My Lord. I shall be returning to Martindale myself later." He nodded and smiled to each man and left the drawing room.

An interesting morning! Cornelius made his way back to his room, pondering the events of the past few hours.

Chatting to his Chief Constable over lunch, both men agreed that it was a rather distasteful end to what had been a pleasant experience.

Armstrong and Baker then met Alex Strickland and his maid Violet at three o'clock on the front steps – the hour agreed, as it was the earliest that James the chauffer would be available to take the three back to Penrith. Baker was due to catch the train back to Carlisle, while Strickland would host Cornelius and his cousin George for dinner that night.

"As the Rolls is not on top form, gentlemen," said James greeting the three, "we will be taking the Mercedes Benz."

"Bloody Germans again," mumbled Strickland to himself.

Although it was out of earshot of the enthusiastic driver, his two companions heard the comment that prompted them to exchange glances. They had agreed to keep the threat to the Kaiser to themselves, but their policemen's instincts could not prevent them mentally going through the guest list to see if there were any obvious candidates. Neither man seriously believed Strickland could be guilty of such nonsense, but both men had a niggling concern about the young Doctor's unhealthy Germanaphobic comments.

Armstrong attempted to lighten Strickland's mood by changing the subject, and, motioning towards his camel-coloured overcoat that had a dark velvet collar said, "That's a nice coat you're wearing Alex."

"Yes, thank you," replied the Doctor, instinctively reaching out an arm to admire it himself, "my parents bought it for my birthday."

James was oblivious to the exchange and concluded his introduction to the Mercedes, with a wave to the sparkling silver vehicle."It was presented to the Earl by the Kaiser when he was here last."

The passengers took their seats while the chauffer strapped their belongings to the vehicle. Once he climbed into the driver's seat, Henry Baker – seated in the front passenger seat – said, "It certainly is a beautiful automobile."

Cornelius Armstrong sat behind his superior officer and rolled his eyes, fearing this was an invitation for James to give a potted history of *this* vehicle, as he had with the Rolls Royce, after picking him up the previous day. It wasn't as bad as Cornelius had feared.

"Yes, I'm very fortunate to be in this job sir, driving these wonderful machines," said James in response. "This is slightly bigger than the Rolls. The Earl has just told me to use this on Thursday when we go to Penrith for the gala dinner – it's now at the *George Hotel* apparently."

Both Baker and Armstrong silently nodded their approval as James released the clutch and the tyres began to crunch the gravel drive beneath them.

Baker said his farewells to Strickland at the railway station, and Armstrong said he would see him back in Carlisle on the following Monday morning. James then took his remaining passengers the short distance to Angel Lane and to Strickland's home and surgery.

The Doctor showed his guest into his study where they found his housekeeper making up a fire.

"Ah Mrs. Brownlee," said Strickland, "this is my friend Cornelius Armstrong who will be staying for dinner tonight. We will be joined by his cousin George who will be arriving by train in an hour or so."

"Hello, sir," said the housekeeper to Cornelius. The news didn't seem to come as a surprise to her, so Armstrong surmised that Strickland had notified her at the time he had contacted George earlier. "I'll make some tea, sir," added Mrs. Brownlee.

Alex and Cornelius chatted for a while over their drink when the clock in the hallway struck five. "I better go and pick George up," said Strickland, "I arranged for my father to have his car brought round earlier."

"Can you manage to drive?" asked Armstrong, with a nod to the young man's leg.

"Yes, I can just about manage short distances," he replied, reaching for his coat. "I'll be back in twenty minutes or so. Make yourself at home."

He hadn't been gone long before the housekeeper returned, "I forgot about the fire, sir! I hope you're not too chilly?"

"No it's fine Mrs. Brownlee, don't worry yourself."

She proceeded to fill the base of the grate with newspaper and kindling.

"You know," said Armstrong watching her, "that's what I am missing at my little cottage in Martindale. I'm trying to make a fire with logs and struggling to get the thing started. Don't tell my own housekeeper, Mrs. Wheeler – I'll never live it down!"

"Your secret's safe with me sir!" said Mrs. Brownlee as she left.

Cornelius began idly looking round Strickland's study. On the wall hung various pictures and memorabilia of his sporting and military exploits; pride of place hung a framed red rugby shirt with a legend embroidered around the badge which read *Cumberland Rugby Football Union 1899*.

As his eye wandered along the wall, it settled on a picture of a group of soldiers outside a building. Under the picture, the legend read *The Volunteers' Blockhouse, South Africa, 1900*.

"Hey, hey!" Cornelius spotted his cousin George in the picture.

The smile was wiped from his face as he turned to go back to his seat;

the top draw of Strickland's desk was ajar, and Armstrong couldn't help noticing an Army Service Revolver inside that was lying next to what looked like a box of bullets.

The Volunteers

The first time Sergeant George Armstrong met *Private* Alex Strickland was in the early months of 1900. The twenty two year old Strickland was one of the Penrith Volunteers selected to join the Border Regiment in their fight against the Boers in South Africa, and George Armstrong was his platoon sergeant.

Many had their doubts about taking volunteers to war but needs must in the Cape, as the regulars were taking a real pounding, and it was decreed in Westminster that the part-timers should bolster the numbers. A company from Carlisle, Kendal and Penrith formed a Volunteer Battalion therefore, and became part of 5,000 volunteers who found themselves on the high seas heading for the Cape during March 1900.

Private Strickland had received news that he was one of the lucky ones in the early days of the new century, and joining him were his best friends Dan Sanderson and Joe Lennon. The young, middle-class, trainee Doctor was from a very different background from his two working class colleagues – both of whom were cabinet makers – but the three had first become friends in their school days through their excelling at rugby.

Despite them all being relatively diminutive figures, all were outstanding players and – after first playing against one another for their respective schools – they simultaneously gravitated to the senior county team by the time they were nineteen. Alex played scrum half, Dan played fly half, while Joe occupied one of the wing three quarter positions. And with their natural sense of adventure, they all joined the volunteers a year later.

A week after hearing about the outbreak of the war from the science master at school, Strickland was with his volunteer colleagues at their annual shooting competition at the Troutbeck Ranges. Strickland would always distinguish himself with a pistol, but was hopeless with a rifle, something for which he was mercilessly ribbed by Dan, Joe, and the rest of his colleagues.

Between then and Christmas, the young men slaked their thirst for knowledge of the war by pouring over the newspapers daily; and when it was suggested part-time soldiers would be required to augment the forces, they couldn't hide their eagerness to be part of the adventure.

When details were released of the dozen men who would represent the town, they instantly became local celebrities: concerts given in their honour, presentations of gifts, and articles about them in the *Herald*. But the heady mix of notoriety, the anticipation of adventure, and the foolishness of youth saw Alex coerce his fiancé Adelaide into joining him in making some unfortunate decisions during that Christmas period; decisions that were to prove bitter sweet in the months to come.

With two months before departure, the young men were sent for training to Carlisle, and once the many route marches round Rickerby, Wetheral and Brisco were under their belts, and the endless sessions of shooting practice on Bitts Park were completed, their time had come.

During their emotional send off, Alex thought his beloved Adelaide was a little subdued, but put it down simply to the occasion and the natural worry experienced by those any soldier leaves behind. His parents were a little more stoic but no less worried.

His two friends had to endure similar discomfort; as far as Dan Sanderson was concerned he only had his mother and younger sister there to see him off, his father having passed away some years earlier. Joe Lennon, being an only one, had his parents offering their worried looks to him on the station platform. Once the traumatic goodbyes were over, the lads were their take-on-the-world ebullient selves again as their troop-carrier sped south to their rendezvous with the *SS Nineveh* in Southampton harbour.

It was the task of the Sergeant George Armstrong of the British Army to keep their young charges busy during the six-week voyage with parades on deck, physical exercise and sports contests. Armstrong quickly noticed that the three young men from Penrith not only had camaraderie between them but displayed intelligence and a maturity that set them aside from most of their colleagues. Strickland in particular caught the Sergeant's eye as being potential Non-Commissioned Officer material should he choose to apply himself in the right areas.

As the men crossed the equator and headed towards the Cape, they didn't realise that not only were they increasingly distancing themselves from their homes, they now had no access to newspapers and therefore had no knowledge of the progress of the war. Once they disembarked at Port Elizabeth, their awareness of the strategic position virtually evaporated as they were instructed to join the long march towards Pretoria.

Reality started to bite for Private Strickland within a week; in his first letter home to Addy he tried to put a brave face on the dusty conditions, the temperatures that soared towards 100°, and its contrast with the sub-zero temperatures which he had experienced during their training marches around Carlisle less than four months earlier.

The banter amongst the troops lessened as the trudge up country continued. Had it not been for Sergeant Armstrong's encouragement and inspiration, the volunteers amongst the group would have struggled to continue.

When their first encounter with the enemy occurred, the battalion was filled with a mixture of relief and excitement. Alex, Dan and Joe were soon to realise that this was a long way – both literally and figuratively – from the Troutbeck Ranges.

The men from Cumberland came under heavy fire from Boer Artillery; Armstrong ordered the volunteers to form a support on the left of the firing line. As they advanced to within 500 yards of the enemy position, Private Strickland's enthusiasm got the better of him and became detached from his platoon.

Sergeant Armstrong instructed his men to get some rapid fire down in order to cover Strickland's vulnerable position. His action proved successful, allowing his stray man back into the fold, and without losing any momentum drove the platoon forward across a dried-up river bed and joined the front firing line in crashing into the enemy positions.

After an hour that saw the three friends fighting shoulder to shoulder under the command of the inspirational NCO, the Boers finally retreated from their positions. It was the first time the Cumbrian soldiers suspected external support for the enemy, as German weapons and ammunition were found in the deserted Boer camp following their hasty exit.

When night fell, the exhilarated soldiers bivouacked on the hills vacated by their enemy. Sanderson and Lennon couldn't help but liken their day's advance to that of some of their successful rugby games.

For his part, the deep-thinking Strickland reflected on his own actions and that of Armstrong and his colleagues who rescued his position. He spent some time talking over the day's events with his sergeant. With two hundred miles of marching and his first encounter with the enemy behind him, he had learned a great deal about soldiering and he was determined to improve.

Finally, the regiment entered the Transvaal capital in mid-July, and learned that the focus of the war had changed: whereas all the other major cities were now in British hands, the Boer *Kommandos* changed their tactics to that of hijacking British supply trains, stealing provisions, and then blending into the small villages and homesteads throughout the Cape, undetectable to their enemy.

All of this seemed insignificant to Private Strickland when he received a letter from home from Addy, informing him that she was expecting his baby. His concern about the stigma that his beloved was enduring back home was overwhelmed by his own selfish euphoria at the news. Sergeant Armstrong turned a blind eye to Alex and his friends letting off steam that night with some of the local brew flowing in great measure. With the war seemingly over, and Strickland's attention turning to home, his hope was that he and his colleagues would be returning soon.

But with the Boers' hit-and-run tactics prolonging matters, the authorities ordered the building of blockhouse look-out posts at mile intervals across the high veldt; and with the part-timers only six months into their twelve-month period of service, they were ordered to move up country to build a blockhouse, near Kroonstadt, almost two hundred miles north of Pretoria.

Before the march – let alone the construction – was completed, morale amongst the men plummeted. Prisoners had been picked up along the way and had to be housed, while the weather lurched from incessant rain to searing heat.

Strickland dreamed of Addy and home, and wrote constantly, barely attempting to disguise his frustration. The only bright spot in the period was the completion of the blockhouse and the day of celebration that went with it, which included the battalion lining up outside of their construction to have the customary picture taken. Little did Private Strickland know, as he posed with his colleagues, that he would be leaving them behind within a few weeks and getting his wish to return home, albeit in heart-breaking circumstances.

Reunions and Reflections

Sergeant George Armstrong was dressed in his civilian clothes as he got off the train at Penrith Station. Alex Strickland recognised his former NCO immediately from where he was standing further down the narrow platform.

"George!" he called, waving above the bobbing heads of other alighting or boarding passengers, and their family or friends, there to meet them or bid them farewell. George looked up over the hubbub and saw Strickland; he waved his acknowledgement.

When the crowd had thinned, the two made their way towards one another and greeted each other with a firm handshake. "It's good to see you again George," said the young Doctor.

"It's good to see you too, Alex – and in better shape than last time, I'm pleased to say."

It had been ten years since Sergeant Armstrong had visited his former subordinate. Strickland's volunteer colleagues had returned to England once their 12-month spell of duty was completed. Armstrong however – being a regular – remained in the Cape until the war's conclusion, and returned with the Regiment in the summer of 1902, a full eighteen months after Strickland had been transported home aboard the hospital ship *The Princess of Wales*.

Upon *his* return, Armstrong made a point of travelling to Penrith to visit the former volunteer who had impressed him so much during their brief service together.

George was aware that Strickland's leg had to be urgently amputated before he left the camp and knew that it would have been a devastating blow to the sportsman and soldier. What he didn't know however, was that Strickland's fiancé and unborn child had been lost at around the same time. When he visited Strickland therefore, he found him in a sanatorium, a near-broken man still trying to come to terms with the previous two years.

After an hour of inane, one-sided conversation, a shocked Armstrong left the Penrithian reflecting on how the person he knew as an energetic, enthusiastic and mischievous individual, was now little more than a shell.

Sergeant Armstrong then resumed his regimental duties at the depot in Carlisle before serving a twelve-month tour of duty in India two years later. With the passing of time and Armstrong's subsequent encounters with scores of other soldiers, his recollections of Strickland's service and its aftermath seeped into his unconsciousness.

That was until Corporal Robins came looking for him twenty-four hours earlier, informing him there was a telephone message for him from a former colleague of his in South Africa. George was amazed and delighted to find it was Strickland who had seemingly recovered from his traumas of a decade earlier. When he learned that Alex had found success in his career, qualifying as a Doctor, and he had coincidentally run into his cousin and best friend Cornelius, he jumped at the chance of travelling down to Penrith to spend some time with them.

As he met Alex on the platform and the two stood shaking hands, the challenges and the memories of the last ten years flashed through both their minds – no words were necessary.

"It's been a long time," George said at last.

"Too long," said Alex.

"I did visit some years ago..," Armstrong stopped himself, not wishing to open up mental scars unnecessarily.

"Did you? That was kind of you. I'm afraid I wasn't on my best form following my return from South Africa."

The soldier smiled and nodded uncomfortably.

"Anyway," resumed Alex, indicating towards his father's motor car, which was parked nearby, "that's all in the past now; shall we get back to my house? Cornelius will be waiting and I know my housekeeper Mrs. Brownlee has cooked us something special for the evening."

"That sounds like a good idea," said George, happy to put the past behind them.

The journey took less than five minutes.

"Fancy meeting you here!" said George upon their arrival and seeing his cousin. The two had last seen each other nine days earlier when they had met for their regular Sunday night drink at *The Board*, just round the corner from Cornelius's lodgings in Carlisle.

"Small world!" countered Cornelius with a smile and a handshake.

Once Alex had introduced his housekeeper and the maid, the three men sat down for dinner around half past six.

"So tell me again," said George, "how did you both meet? I didn't really catch the gist on the telephone."

Alex simply answered, "I was introduced to Lord Lonsdale by a professional colleague." He then recited how the Earl and the Kaiser were friends and as the German party was visiting, the Earl had invited him along to the gathering at Lowther Castle. "Seeming intent on seeing a few locals jump through hoops for him," was Strickland's barbed conclusion to his narrative, as the maid cleared the soup bowls from the table.

"So, how did you get roped in Corny?" asked the soldier turning to his cousin, "I thought you were supposed to be on holiday?"

"I was!" replied the policeman. "But Henry collared me before I left and I became one of the hoop-jumpers as well I'm afraid."

"Not that I actually did anything while I was there; I only met the Kaiser briefly and even then he didn't ask me anything about police work."

"Nor me," interrupted Alex. "Prig!" He spat the word out with such ferocity it forced the two cousins to swap a quick glance.

Cornelius took the lead in steering the conversation away from the Kaiser's visit by talking about anything, from the weather to the history of St Martin's Church, near his holiday cottage. But inevitably, given the company that night, the conversation continually gravitated back to matters military, whether it was the current arms race throughout Europe, or the war in South Africa all those years ago.

Whenever it did so, Cornelius noticed that Strickland's demeanour changed markedly from that of the relaxed, jovial host, to that of a bitter, angry radical. George seemed not to notice the change in mood, perhaps because of his genuine interest in the topic, but it became quite apparent to his cousin that, as the night went on, Strickland would continually descend into brief periods of gloom whenever German, political, or military matters were discussed.

When the clock struck ten, Cornelius suggested that perhaps it was time for him and George to leave.

"Of course," agreed Alex, "it would be unfair of me to keep you any longer. "Will you be all right driving my father's car, George?"

"Yes, if you trust me!" said the soldier who had been trained in driving various types of military vehicles.

"I'll arrange to get your coats," said Strickland, leaving the room.

A moment later he returned with his housekeeper, who addressed Cornelius, "I took the liberty of making you up a bag of kindling and some newspapers for that fire you were telling me about, sir."

"Thank you, Mrs. Brownlee," said Cornelius laughing, while his two companions looked quizzically on. "Where would we be without a good housekeeper to look after us?"

The cousins thanked their hosts once again and set off back to Cornelius's Martindale hideaway in the borrowed motor car. When they had left the outskirts of Penrith and there was a pause in the desultory conversation, Cornelius asked, "What did you think of Alex's demeanour tonight?"

"It was much better than I expected to be honest," replied George. He went on to explain some of the events in South Africa and his subsequent visit to the convalescing Strickland following his return. "If you'd told me then he'd be a qualified, successful Doctor a few years later, I wouldn't have believed you," he concluded.

"Still," said Cornelius, "I was worried about some of his behaviour towards the Germans at Lowther. And then again tonight – every time the conversation veered towards politics or the military, it was as though a dark cloud descended over him."

"Can't say I really noticed," said George. "Mind you, I do remember those Penrith lads in South Africa and their loathing of Germans. They were all convinced they were behind the Boers; and when Alex got wounded it made the remainder even worse, so convinced were they of German involvement.

"I remember there was a preacher or a pastor or something, who visited the Boer prisoners. What was his name again…? Anyway, some of the volunteers – especially the Penrith lads – were convinced he was up to no good." He thought for a while, trying to remember the preacher's name.

"There is something I didn't tell you, George, I didn't want to raise it in front of Alex. When we were at Lowther there was a threat made against the Kaiser. A crude anti-German note had been made with cuttings from an old newspaper."

George turned his head and looked at his cousin for longer than he should have before turning his eyes back towards the road, "You don't suspect Alex do you?"

"I don't know," replied the policeman. "All of my instincts say it can't be but increasingly, the circumstantial evidence suggests it may *well* be."

"Why would he risk everything he's worked for?" asked the soldier, almost to himself.

Cornelius exhaled through his nose, as puzzled as his cousin. "I don't know," he said shaking his head.

They drove on in silence for some time, contemplating the conversation.

"You've got me thinking back to South Africa now Corny," said George at last. "As I say, there was anti-German feeling among the lads then, but could it fester for this long? I keep thinking about that preacher – what *was* his name again…?

The Decline of Alex Strickland

Weiss. The name George was trying to remember was that of Reverend Alfred Weiss. The first time Sergeant Armstrong and his men encountered him was the week after they had completed building the blockhouse at Kroonstadt. The Reverend Weiss turned up at the camp with a request to give some pastoral care to the Boer prisoners being held by the Border men.

The Commanding Officer, Captain Vaughan, didn't see anything wrong with the request and believed it would help defuse any tension between the prisoners and his men. Weiss thereafter made regular – apparently uneventful – visits to the camp. But when his brethren within the camp started to grow significantly, their captors began to suspect that all was not as it seemed. When Private Sanderson saw him from a distance handing something to one of the Boers, his suspicions were fuelled still further.

He quickly reported his observations to Sergeant Armstrong. "Sarge, that German's been giving something to the Boers."

"How do you mean?" asked the NCO.

"I just saw him handing something to one of prisoners. I couldn't see what it was from where I was standing, but the Boer looked this way and that – it all looked a bit odd if you ask me."

Just then, Weiss's wagonette rattled past on its way out of the camp. "Reverend!" called Sergeant Armstrong looking up, "what were you handing to the prisoners?"

"Just bibles," said Weiss, without halting his pony, "what else could it be? I am spreading the word of God."

The two soldiers watched him go, unimpressed with either his answer or his dismissive manner. When the resultant search of the site turned up nothing, the Volunteers were somewhat assuaged, but the remaining tension that hung over the base camp was palpable.

The mood of the Battalion wasn't helped when, a few weeks later, news reached them that scheduled peace talks designed to bring an end to the war had failed. The Boer leaders steadfastly refused to give up their country's independence. In an effort to pound their enemy into submission, the British burned the locals' farmsteads and housed women and children in concentration camps. Boer guerrillas retaliated by attacking the camps.

The Border Regiment had already re-buffed three such attacks in as many weeks when Private Alex Strickland found himself on night guard duty in June 1901. It was dawn when two Boer prisoners appeared from one of the cabins and approached the soldier, who was guarding the entrance to their enclosure with a regular colleague, Private Jack Walker.

"What are those two up to?" said Strickland as he saw them coming.

Walker looked up and left his colleague to approach them. He was about ten yards from Strickland, who remained at the entrance, when he was knocked off his feet by an almighty crash. A shell had exploded behind him; it was the signal for the prisoners to come pouring out of their cabins and charge towards the entrance where mounted Boer guerrillas appeared from nowhere. Soldiers countered by running from their quarters in various states of undress whilst wrestling with their rifles.

Explosions and arms fire filled the air as Boers and British fought over the tiny spot of veldt. It was all over in a matter of minutes, and as horses galloped away it became apparent that some of the prisoners were lost. As the others were re-captured, it was Dan Sanderson who saw his friend Alex Strickland lying unconscious by his post – Sanderson thought he was dead. He rushed over and carried out some basic checks; his helmet and part of his uniform had been blown off revealing a virtually naked upper body that was charred black and caked in blood and sweat. Fortunately, Private Sanderson found his friend to be breathing.

"*MEDICAL ASSISTANCE!*" screamed Dan over his shoulder.

It was only when Joe Lennon and three other colleagues ran over to help lift the wounded soldier that it became evident to Sanderson that

Strickland's left leg had been badly injured. What looked like part of the shinbone appeared to be peeping through the soldier's ripped puttee. "CAREFUL!" he screamed at his colleagues as they went to lift the man onto a makeshift stretcher.

The Penrith Volunteer was carried to the 'hospital' which was a room in one of the temporary buildings. Lieutenant Miles, the Chief Medical Officer, directed the men to lay him out on one of the tables and set about cutting the rest of his uniform away. His left leg was split in several places and, with the modest facilities available in the field hospital, Miles took little time in deciding that it had to be removed there and then to prevent gangrene setting in.

Within two days of the emergency operation taking place, and with the wounded soldier still sedated, he was transferred onto a troop-carrying train and sent to Port Elizabeth where he was loaded onto the hospital ship *The Princess of Wales* bound for home.

The six-week voyage to England was long, painful and depressing for the young man who was still trying to come to terms with his life-changing disability. When he arrived, and found the double tragedy of his fiancé and unborn child being lost, he immediately sank into a depression from which his parents believed he would never recover.

Dan Sanderson tried to keep in contact with his friend through his sister and with several letters, but Strickland refused to see anyone and couldn't muster the energy or the inclination to write. When his volunteer colleagues returned home a few months later, Strickland wondered long and hard whether he should go to the station or not to meet them.

Penrith was in a high state of excitement as news of the Volunteers' return became known. On the day itself, a pre-arranged siren from the Gas Works shrieked at the imminent arrival of the local heroes as the station clock ticked past midday.

After much persuasion from his parents, the fragile Alex decided to go and meet his friends, but as the train came into view amid a crescendo of fog horns, ringing cheers, and waving hats from the thousands of onlookers in and around the station, the crowd and the noise became too much for him and he demanded his father return them home.

Instead, he read about the homecoming the following day in *The Herald*, with its pomp, circumstance and joyous scenes: the Penrith soldiers marched through the wall of noise along King Street towards Market Square, where a platform had been constructed for the men in front of the Liverpool Bank, while the town's dignitaries gave speeches from the first floor windows above.

After receiving various souvenirs from the Mayor, the men joined their townsfolk in singing the national anthem before going to the home of their Commanding Officer, Lieutenant Haswell, where a small reception was held and a final photograph was taken on the lawn outside. The picture was printed in the newspaper and Alex was left staring at it, alone with his thoughts.

Rather than provide a fillip for the recovering soldier, the homecoming of his colleagues appeared to cause greater anxiety, and it wasn't long before he was transferred to the sanatorium on Beacon Hill to further aid his recovery.

The war finally ended the following year, the regulars from the Border Regiment returned home, and the Volunteers travelled to Manchester to receive their campaign medals from Lord Roberts: all events that passed Strickland by.

His friends and colleagues regularly visited him, and did their best to aid his recovery, but it was left to the man himself over the following two years to come to terms with not only his disability, but the inner-demons that continued to torment him following his return from South Africa.

Alex finally left the sanatorium in late 1904, and with the encouragement and guidance from his father, he resumed his medical studies and qualified as a Doctor the following year. He worked as the junior partner at his father's town-centre surgery for a further two years before the elder Strickland announced that he was to retire and leave Alex in sole charge of the business, while he and Alex's mother moved to a small house on the outskirts of town.

The plans of Doctor Strickland senior were almost dashed three months before he was about to handover when his son fell into a bout of deep depression following another tragedy, but Alex's mind cleared and the arrangement with him and his father came to fruition in early 1906. His confidence and mental health had steadily improved following the transition – that was until the Kaiser's visit seven years later.

Suspicions Confirmed

George Armstrong left his cousin Cornelius the following morning. They had completed the rest of their journey from Penrith to Martindale in relative silence following their conversation about Alex Strickland and his outspoken views on the German visitors.

Both were a little disturbed by their observations, but equally both struggled to believe that Strickland was capable of violence against the Kaiser.

Once they were back at the small cottage Cornelius was renting for the week, the policeman poured them each a glass of rum from the bottle which he had packed for his trip. The two chatted for a while before turning in.

George had made arrangements to return the motor car to Alex's surgery before catching the lunchtime train to Carlisle where he would resume his duties that afternoon at the castle.

The two shook hands and agreed to meet as usual at *The Board* on Sunday, once Cornelius had returned from his holiday.

For his part, although Cornelius enjoyed the company of his cousin immensely, he was pleased to be finally on his own in the isolation of the North Lakes. It had been a strangely long week so far, full of activities the would-be holiday maker could never have predicted. Now, Armstrong was determined to fill the last three days of his holiday with the walking, reading and solitude he had promised himself in the first place.

It was approaching ten o'clock by the time George left, so Cornelius decided to make a quick sandwich and set off walking immediately following his departure rather than spend time building a fire for later and cleaning up before setting off, by which time half the day would be lost.

He still intended to take on Helvellyn, but knew that he would have had to make an earlier start for the all-day hike up the high peak. Instead, he decided to simply get out and follow his nose, believing that it was the activity itself which was important this particular day and not necessarily the content nor the sense of achievement.

It proved just the tonic for the off-duty policeman who had become a little bemused by the events of the previous few days. He had little difficulty putting the Kaiser and his hangers-on to the back of his mind; the thought of Alex and his erratic manner could not be dismissed quite so easily, however. The Army Service Revolver he accidentally spotted in Strickland's desk drawer particularly bothered him.

Over dinner, George had brought up the subject of shooting at one point and teased Alex about his poor marksmanship with a rifle. Strickland replied that he always believed it was because he was left-handed and the larger weapon didn't lend itself to a 'lefty.' He supported the argument by emphasising his proficiency with the hand-held revolver. "Can't argue with that," replied George, "best pistol shot in the battalion."

Did Alex just keep the gun as a memento? But if he was so bitter about the war, why would he have anything that reminded him of it?

It was three o'clock in the afternoon by the time Cornelius returned to his cottage. After a little cleaning up and washing some pots from earlier, he intended on building a fire, in front of which he proposed to spend the rest of the afternoon and evening engrossed in *The Moonstone*, a book that had been on his 'to do' list for some time.

No sooner had he cleared the dishes away when there was a knock at the door. "What now?" he growled.

He opened the door to find Ned Matthews, the farmer from down the valley whom he had met at church the previous Sunday.

"Hello Mr Armstrong, I am just going into Pooley Bridge for a few things. I wondered if you wanted anything."

Cornelius had been so wrapped up in his own thoughts he hadn't heard Matthews's vehicle as it chugged towards the cottage. "Ned! How kind of you – I don't think there is, thank you all the same."

The two chatted for a few minutes before bidding each other farewell and promising they would meet again before the policeman left on Saturday. As Armstrong closed the door he felt a little guilty that Matthews had taken the time to call, which meant that he had to unnecessarily stop and – more significantly – try to re-start his temperamental vehicle.

He walked over to the fire and reached for the kindling and papers which Mrs. Brownlee had given him. Taking the newspapers he started to tear individual sheets and twist them into what his mother used to call 'bows' before placing them in the grate and laying some kindling on top.

After ripping up the first two cover sheets of the newspaper, he absentmindedly noticed that a tiny cut had been made halfway down the following page, creating a small hole in the particular news story. Carrying on without giving the matter a thought, he stared in horror two pages later when he discovered that a full-page spread on the Kaiser's visit had been reduced to near shreds: individual words from the headline and grouped words within the text had been cut from the page.

At a glance, Cornelius could deduce the words *Kaiser; German; good;* and *dead* were all missing. Armstrong assumed that the tiny cutting from the previous pages had provided words which were not available as part of this main feature but he felt that he didn't need any further confirmation: *the threat against the Kaiser had originated from Strickland. Whatsmore, the Earl might be leading his guest into grave danger tonight, as the Gala Dinner is due to take place a few hundred yards from Strickland's house.*

He suddenly became aware of the sound of Ned Matthews's vehicle pulling away; he jumped up and ran out of the cottage calling to the farmer – a futile course of action given the variety of banging and clattering noises which were emanating from Ned's vehicle. As it bumped and rocked its way up the dusty track, Cornelius sprinted after it and managed to bang on the back of the wagon with the palm of his hand, prompting the farmer to stop.

"Ned!" called Armstrong again, running up to the front of the vehicle, "something's happened. I need to go to Pooley Bridge after all. Do I recall you saying that the Postmistress has a telephone there?"

"That's right sir," said Matthews, more than a little surprised by the sudden change of mind.

"Well in that case, if the offer is still open?"

"Of course," said Ned, "you're more than welcome sir."

Cornelius dashed back for his coat. Re-emerging a few seconds later, he locked the door, "I really appreciate this Ned," he said as he climbed into the cramped cab of the vehicle.

"That's all right sir."

"Please, call me Cornelius."

"Very well sir," said Ned instinctively.

Armstrong smiled but chose not to pursue it.

The journey down The Hause and through Howtown was bumpy, but Cornelius hoped it would prove a worthwhile trip. He intended to call Strickland and confront him with his suspicions. If they were true then he hoped to dissuade Alex from pursuing such a stupid course of action. If he couldn't connect with Strickland then he would attempt to call Lowther Castle and speak with the Earl before he and his guest left for Penrith.

His plans were dashed however when they arrived at Pooley Bridge. To his immense frustration he discovered that the telephone was not working due to a fault at the exchange. He turned to Matthews upon learning of the news from the apologetic Postmistress.

"Ned, I have an enormous favour to ask..."

The Ticking Clock

Thursday evening was to be the first time that the Kaiser would leave the grounds of Lowther Castle since he had spoken with the policeman from Carlisle the previous Monday. He and his staff had grown bored, and were looking forward to the following day when they were to leave for home. Even Lord Lonsdale had lost his enthusiasm for their visit – no hunting and little fun. Surely the advice from Baker's man was a little extreme, but there was a small voice in his head which told him it was better to be safe than sorry.

He had reflected that the safest of all courses of action would be to host the evening at the castle itself, but that was never an option as the Countess had already arranged to entertain her Conservative colleagues from the Primrose League that same evening.

So when half past six arrived on that Thursday evening, there was an air of going through the motions on the one hand, and a certain relief at a change of setting on the other. James the chauffer carried the Earl, Kaiser and his personal bodyguard in the Mercedes Benz, while the rest of Wilhelm's entourage followed in a four-car motorcade behind.

As they passed through the villages on the way to Penrith, locals in their ones-and-twos lined the roadside to catch a glimpse of the unusual sight. By the time they reached the town itself some twenty minutes later, hundreds of spectators stood by the roadside waving and applauding their illustrious guests. The cars slowed in sight of the *George Hotel* where the Lord Lieutenant of Cumberland and the other distinguished guests were already waiting.

Approximately thirty minutes after their grand arrival into Penrith, another – less distinguished – vehicle chugged into the town from the south. The driver continued to involuntarily bounce up and down in his seat, believing any ceasing of his movement would jeopardise the forward momentum of his motorised cart. His passenger meanwhile sat in an anxious silence, hoping that the vehicle would continue for just a little longer, and that he would find his nervousness regarding the intentions of his Penrith friend, were misplaced. He was now reasonably confident of the former, but he was becoming increasingly uncertain of the latter.

Once the monument was in sight in the centre of the town, Cornelius Armstrong gave Ned Matthews his final directions, "Turn left up here, Ned, and then onto Angel Lane."

The farmer was clearly nervous of driving in the built-up area and took extra care along the unfamiliar streets, before turning onto the road suggested by his passenger.

"Just here on the right," ordered the policeman, who was already wrestling with the temperamental door handle on the passenger side of the vehicle. As he did so, he didn't see the figure hastily leaving the surgery.

Ned leaned over his passenger and rattled the handle until it released the catch, allowing Armstrong to hop out of the truck and bound up the few steps to the front door of Strickland's surgery. With a staccato rap of the door knocker he waited patiently, trying to convince himself that he was being stupid and his over-active imagination would end up causing him a great deal of embarrassment.

Finally, Mrs. Brownlee opened the door, "Oh, Mr Armstrong, sir," she said standing aside to welcome the visitor, "what a pleasant surprise. Doctor Strickland never said you were coming."

"No, that's right Mrs. Brownlee," said Cornelius entering and immediately looking around the hallway towards Strickland's study, "it is a bit of an unscheduled visit. Could I ask if the Doctor is in this evening?"

"No he went out earlier, sir – didn't say where. I heard the door go a few minutes ago and thought that was him coming back but he's not here."

"I'm sorry Mrs. Brownlee, but can I just check something in the Doctor's study?" Armstrong didn't wait for the housekeeper's permission before opening the door. He went over to the desk drawer – the contents of which had caused him so much concern earlier in the week – and opened it.It was empty!

"Damn! The gun!" cried Armstrong, forgetting his company for a moment; and then to the housekeeper, "The gun, Mrs. Brownlee, do you know where the Doctor's gun is?"

The poor woman looked completely bemused by the policeman's outburst.Not waiting for a response, Armstrong rushed past the housekeeper, convinced that his friend's jaundiced view of the Kaiser and his countrymen had led him towards a catastrophic decision. As he ran through the hallway, the clock chimed the quarter hour. "'The George!'" Armstrong shouted to no one in particular and he ran out of the house and bounded down the steps onto the street.

Running down Angel Lane and onto King Street in a matter of seconds, he looked across the sixty-or-so yards to the entrance of the *George Hotel*, and saw Strickland in his distinctive camel-coloured coat and black hat crossing the threshold of the main entrance and disappearing from view.

Too late, he thought as he sprinted across the road.

Inside the hotel, the guests had just been served their soup, when Von Gering, the Kaiser's equerry, excused himself to visit the wash rooms. As he left the dining room, he almost collided with the diminutive figure that had just walked in. The unexpected occurrence caught the German by surprise, and the oddity of someone walking into the dining room wearing their coat with the collar turned up and their hat pulled down flitted through Von Gering's mind, but his natural momentum carried him out of the room without giving the matter further consideration.

Then, an explosion of confusion, fear and shock filled the air as Von Gering heard the commotion of a man bursting through the main entrance of the hotel. Turning, he saw a man who was running towards him through the foyer – he seemed vaguely familiar.

Cornelius Armstrong recognised the equerry standing in the doorway of the dining room and feared he was too late. Barging past him through the doorway, he instantly felt the atmosphere crackling with tension and confusion as the scores of guests began to sense that something was terribly wrong.

Amid the noise of the muffled shrieks and disturbed tableware, Armstrong saw the assassin walking towards the top table, at which sat Kaiser Wilhelm. He saw the barrel of the revolver peeping out from the right sleeve of the coat. The policeman lunged forward as the gun was being raised, less than ten feet from its intended victim who sat there paralysed, not knowing what he was seeing.

Armstrong flung out his right hand and grabbed the barrel of the gun and, as the struggle began, he managed to twist it upwards towards the ceiling.

For a heart-stopping instant – that bizarrely appeared to happen in slow motion from Armstrong's point of view – the muzzle of the gun passed in front of his face. Almost simultaneously, the gun discharged twice in quick succession. Unknown to Armstrong at the time, one of the bullets grazed the side of his face before smashing into a chandelier. It shattered raining shards of crystal down onto the protagonists below and forced screams from the guests, who were now either barging into each other in a confused effort to get out, or seeking refuge under the dining tables.

Four hands grappled with the revolver before the assassin managed to yank it towards him. Cornelius momentarily lost his grip and was almost overcome with fear, knowing he was in mortal danger if the killer could set and fire. The sudden pulling motion of his opponent, however, inadvertently generated some forward momentum for Armstrong, and instead of diving for cover he took advantage of it and grabbed his enemy once more, just as a third, uncontrolled, shot was discharged into one of the pillars of the ornate room.

He got a new grip on the barrel of the gun, and managed to drive the killer towards the wall and steer the muzzle of the gun downwards. The two wrestled their way back towards the centre of the room as their death-struggle continued.

After what seemed like an eternity, but what must have been only a few seconds, finally a fourth shot was fired. Suddenly both contestants stopped grappling and stood totally still, hanging on to one another, not entirely sure what had just happened. Cornelius was wrenched from his paralysis by the sound of someone screaming a name. In a semi-dazed state, he turned to see Alex Strickland standing in the doorway of the dining room.

"*VIOLET!*" screamed Strickland again.

The disbelieving Armstrong turned back to his opponent. For a second they stood in silence before he realised the eyes were wide and unseeing. As the would-be assassin began to slip from his grasp, the hat was dislodged, and locks of long auburn cascaded over the shoulders of Violet Sanderson. Her lifeless body slumped to the floor, with blood seeping from a gunshot wound in her stomach.

The Kaiser's Would-Be Assassin

Cornelius Armstrong and Alex Strickland stood over the body of Violet Sanderson in the dining room of the George Hotel; the room was now virtually empty.

As soon as Violet had raised the gun and it became apparent that this was an assassination attempt, the Kaiser's bodyguard hurled himself in front of Wilhelm, knocking him, the Earl, and the Lord Lieutenant – who were sitting either side of him – to the ground. As the policeman grappled with the would-be killer, the three VIPs were shuffled away through the kitchen and into the vehicles which had been moved to the back of the hotel for the duration of the evening. By the time the commotion was over inside, the dignitaries had been sped away.

Most of the other guests were left to make their own arrangements: it seems they had either found a way out of the maelstrom of violence as it was taking place, or they had emerged from under their tables at its conclusion and left the hotel in shock.

The supine body was now lying in a pool of dark blood amid the debris of broken crockery, cutlery and crystal. Armstrong and Strickland stood in silence looking down, still struggling to take in what happened just a few minutes earlier.

"Cornelius, you're hurt," said Alex at last after raising his head and seeing the blood trickling down the Inspector's cheek.

It was the first that Armstrong knew of the injury; he instinctively reached up to his face and then looked at the blood on his fingertips. "I must have been caught," he said through his dazed state.

Both turned as the Vicar from nearby St Andrew's Church came hurrying into the room – he had been alerted to the commotion within minutes and made the short journey along the street to see if he could offer any help. "Gentlemen, I heard the terr-" he stopped in his tracks when he saw the body of the young woman lying in the middle of the floor. "Good heavens! It seems I am too late to offer any assistance."

"Thank you Reverend," said Strickland, "but I'm afraid it *is* too late."

"Perhaps I could arrange some tea?"

The comment was typically English, but sounded wholly appropriate to Cornelius who was still trying to come to terms with what had happened. "That would be much appreciated, thank you," he said.

As the Vicar left the room, the two sat down at a nearby table, trying to take it all in.

"I thought it was you, Alex." Armstrong was not only in shock following his struggle with the killer, he was still surprised that it was not the Doctor he had been wrestling with.

Strickland looked at the policeman blankly, then suddenly realised why his friend would think that: his attitude during their stay at Lowther Castle, and then the impression that he must have created when he hosted the two cousins a couple of nights later. He bowed his head and nodded almost guiltily, wondering if it would have altered events had he behaved differently.

Before he could say anything, a white-clad figure appeared from the kitchen carrying a silver tray on which sat two cups and a pot of tea. The wide-eyed waiter made an arc around the middle of the room trying his best not to look at the corpse. The refreshment contributed to the two regaining a little composure. Strickland gathered himself, feeling the need to provide an explanation.

Earlier that afternoon he had visited a Doctor-friend of his in Kendal. Doctor Steven Goleman specialised in the field of Psychoanalysis, pioneered over the previous two decades on the Continent. Alex had been seeing Goleman in his professional capacity on-and-off for some years. His experiences in South Africa and its tragic aftermath had worn heavily on the young man's nerves, and bouts of depression that lasted for several days were not unfamiliar.

He had experienced a reasonably stable few months until this past week, when his mixing with the Kaiser and his party succeeded in dragging him into a morose pit from which he was struggling to climb out. He had decided to pay Goleman a visit who, fortunately, had an opening and could accommodate the Penrith man at short notice.

"I didn't broadcast my visits to Steven," explained Strickland to the policeman, "I felt a little embarrassed about it in truth. Besides, I didn't want Mrs. Brownlee, let alone my parents, worrying about me unnecessarily."

After some further contemplation, he continued, "I never should have accepted the Earl's damned invitation in the first place. My curiosity overtook my instinct."

"You could never have known it would turn out like this," consoled Cornelius.

"Perhaps not," said Alex, "but I didn't exactly help matters did I?"

As other officials started to arrive to remove the body, the policeman's mind was now turning to the safety of the others who were present earlier, and the young woman's motives for her actions.

It was approaching midnight by the time Violet's body was finally covered and carried out of the dining room of the *George Hotel*. With nothing else that could be done there, Armstrong suggested that he and the Doctor return to Strickland's surgery, where his maid's quarters could be inspected.

By the time they made the short journey back to Angel Lane, Mrs. Brownlee was waiting for them. Her expression clearly indicated that she knew about the events. Strickland said nothing – he simply hugged her and allowed her to sob into his chest.

"Can we see Violet's room?" asked Cornelius after a while.

Strickland led the Inspector down the stairs into the basement where the young woman had her living quarters. Armstrong glanced around the small, modest room. There was a bed, a wardrobe with a set of drawers that didn't match, and a small bureau, beside which stood a chair that seemed to serve the dual purpose of giving its occupant the opportunity to write at the desk, or simply use it in an occasional capacity.

On the open bureau were scattered some papers and what looked like a journal. Mounted on the wall directly above it hung three photographs.

One was a copy of the picture Strickland had in his study: that of the Volunteers outside of the blockhouse in South Africa. The one next to it was of three young soldiers – one of whom Armstrong recognised as Strickland. The third was a picture of one of the other two soldiers with Violet.

The Doctor appeared as surprised as the Inspector when he saw these pictures; it was clear that he had never visited his maid's private quarters before. As the policeman continued to study the photographs, Strickland explained their significance, first pointing to the one of Violet and the young soldier.

"Violet was the younger sister of my friend Dan Sanderson," and then, murmuring to himself, "I've never seen this photograph before. They thought the world of each other, having lost their father when they were just children. Their mother brought them up single-handedly." He then looked at the middle photograph with a rueful smile, "This is me, with Dan and Joe Lennon, shortly after we arrived at the Cape."

"Where's Dan now?" asked Armstrong.

"Dead," was Strickland's curt answer. "He got through the war unscathed, but died suddenly of heart failure in 1905. It was shocking, a young lad in the prime of life; sportsman, soldier – no one could believe it. Poor Violet was with him when he collapsed in the street. Mrs. Sanderson went downhill after that and died herself – I'm sure of a broken heart – within eighteen months.

"Knowing the family as I did, and being so close to Dan, I took Violet in after her mother's death and gave her a job as my maid. She and Mrs. Brownlee got on well together; I never thought her capable of anything like this."

Armstrong moved to the items on the bureau. Newspaper cuttings detailing the Kaiser's visit were mixed haphazardly with letters, removed from their envelopes. The Inspector picked up two of the letters: they were written by Violet's brother in 1901 when he was still in South Africa. Dan Sanderson clearly made no attempt to hide his feelings of despair and anger from his sister. Armstrong picked out some significant sentences from both correspondences:

Dearest Violet…The conditions here are dreadful. Insects and Boers attack us in equal measure…Increasingly, those damn Germans appear to be supplying the enemy with arms to prolong this awful war.

My Darling Sister…When will this conflict ever end? I can't wait to get home and see you again…If it wasn't for the damn Germans, I'm sure it would be all over by now. I blame them for Alex's injury… The only good German is a dead German.

This final comment reminded Armstrong of the crude note that had been left for the Kaiser earlier in the week. *It was obviously Violet who had made the note – possibly before she and Alex had even left for Lowther.*

Armstrong then turned to the maid's journal. She appeared to use it as an outlet for her own demons: anti-German rants were interspersed with melancholy recollections of happier times spent with her brother. In her diary, she also declared her love for her employer and guardian. Reluctantly, Armstrong handed the items to Strickland, who stared at them, incredulous.

"The poor girl," he uttered, "I had no idea. Dan must have planted the seed years ago and the poor girl has carried around the burden ever since, waiting to vent her anger and retribution on someone. And of course, I didn't help, with my pathetic behaviour."

He thought for a little longer. "I've just realised, Violet witnessed my spat with that wretched Fleischer. My humiliation must have fuelled her hatred even more."

Armstrong added, "She was in the car on the way back from Lowther and was party to the chauffer telling us about the change of location for this evening's event. Seeing you go out, she must have seen her opportunity to have her retribution; she took your gun, disguised herself as you, and went to 'The George.'"

Being so late, Armstrong stayed at Strickland's house that night before returning to the cottage the following morning to collect his things prior to leaving for home.

Within twelve months of the Kaiser's visit, the fears of many were realised and the world was drawn into a war that far surpassed the scale of the conflict in South Africa over a decade earlier. As the war to end all wars dragged on, rarely did a day go by when Cornelius didn't wonder about his actions in Penrith that autumn night, and how the course of history might have been altered if the outcome of his struggle with Violent Sanderson had been different.

Historical Note

Dating from the reign of Queen Elizabeth I, the Carlisle Racing Bells and the Cumberland Plate are thought to be the oldest known horseracing prizes in Britain.

The races were the highlight of the leisure calendar in the late nineteenth and early twentieth centuries, when the factories and businesses closed throughout the city for 'Race Week' which took place at the end of June.

The races have taken place for over a hundred years at the current racecourse that was opened at Blackwell at the south of the city in 1904.

Among the fictitious characters in *The Bells and Plate Fix* are two very real people who deserve mention and credit.

Detective Inspector Robert Mather was the Manchester policeman who helped Cornelius Armstrong track down the Glasgow villain Seamus McAllindon. Mather was a visionary detective who kept a scrapbook of known criminals in the early 1900s that could be seen as the forerunner to the computer databases developed by his successors later in the century. Inspector Mather retired from the force in 1921 – his scrapbook was sold at auction for a four-figure sum in 2012.

The second actual character in the story was Joseph Bell, Chief Engineer of *RMS Titanic*, who was born in Farlam near Brampton in 1861.

The young Joseph left Carlisle and went to Newcastle as an apprentice engine fitter at Robert Stephenson's and Co before joining the White Star line in 1885. Working with the company for twenty-five years, he was promoted to Chief Engineer in 1910, serving on the *Coptic* and the *Olympic* before being transferred to the *Titanic* prior to its maiden voyage. Legend has it that he and his men refused to desert their posts as they battled to keep the stricken vessel afloat and to maintain power right up to the last minute. He was one of 1517 to perish in the disaster. His cousin, pathologist James Bell, is my own creation.

I have to concede that I have taken a little poetic licence with my description of *Titanic's* sailing from Queenstown. The account is more in keeping with its original launch from Southampton.

Another very real character of course was Kaiser Wilhelm II of Germany. He was friends with Hugh Cecil Lowther, the 5th Earl of Lonsdale and visited at the Earl's Lowther Castle home on more than one occasion. I am not aware of the Kaiser being threatened during his visits to the county!

Sadly, the Kaiser and the Earl's friendship soured as they ended up on opposing sides when war broke out in 1914. The 11th (Lonsdale) Battalion, The Border Regiment was raised by the Earl in September 1914 and fought with distinction on the Western Front throughout the conflict.

Any dialogue attributed to real people in this volume, and any meetings or events described are my own creation.

Martin Daley

The Casebook of Inspector Armstrong Volume III

Detective Inspector Cornelius Armstrong will return in the third volume of his casebook.

As the nineteenth century draws to its close, a visitor to Carlisle – innocently exploring his family heritage – inadvertently discovers all is not well within the Presbyterian community of the city. *The Young American* brings his concerns to the attention of the authorities, and a case of blackmail and embezzlement becomes one of the first investigations for the newly promoted Inspector Armstrong. Cornelius solves the case and is destined to meet the visitor again; twenty years later as he makes a second visit to the city as the 28th President of the United States.

In the second short novel, war rages across the globe in 1917. Prime Minister Lloyd George builds the giant munitions factory in Gretna in the wake of the Shell Crisis. Law and order become an issue in Carlisle as munitions workers descend on the city during their leisure time, and Lloyd George's 'great experiment' sees the introduction of State Management pubs to control the sale and consumption of alcohol. Just when Inspector Armstrong thinks order has been restored on the streets of the city, he is called to look into an explosion at the factory. His investigations uncover a serious misuse of *The Devil's Porridge* that may not only threaten the proposed visit of King George V and Queen Mary, but could also halt production and jeopardise the allies' progress on the Western Front.